MW01193525

Roll for Initiative
An Indestructibles Story

Matthew Phillion

Roll for Initiative: An Indestructibles Story
Lost Continuity Press
Contact:
theindestructiblesbook@gmail.com
www.theindestructiblesbook.com
December 2017
Printed in the United States of America
© 2017 Matthew Phillion
First Edition: © Matthew Phillion / Lost Continuity Press
ISBN-13: 978-1-9832742-1-3
Cover Design by Sterling Arts and Design:
http://www.sterlingartsanddesign.com

From the Author

A bit of background:

About a year ago I started thinking about taking a break from the Indestructibles to explore a different genre. My attention, of course, turned to fantasy novels, and I began brainstorming about a young adult adventure set in a quasi-medieval setting. My mind of course turned to the characters I'd tell that story about, and I realized very quickly that I wasn't really thinking about a fantasy story... I was imagining the Indestructibles *in* a fantasy story.

Or more accurately, the Indestructibles playing a game of Dungeons & Dragons or Pathfinder.

The classes they'd choose were pretty obvious (though Emily was debatable). Who would have played these types of games before and who would want nothing to do with it was also very clear. But the question was: how do I get them there?

Of course, it would be Emily's fault. It's always Emily's fault.

I also felt like the story would be somewhat out of continuity with the main series, which has a growth arc for the Indestructibles, while this would be the equivalent of a holiday special or a comic book annual. Something that is canon but not plot pivotal to the primary arc. I thought it would be a short story, and thus perfect as a One-Shot as I've started calling these standalone shorts.

By the time they meet their first goblin, I realized this was going to be a novella instead.

I love that tabletop role playing games have become fashionable and mainstream. Sure, there's a little part of me that feels slightly resentful for being made fun of for enjoying these games as a kid, but I'm also glad that people are able to enjoy the things they love freely these days—I feel much the same way about loving superhero stories as I do about role playing games. They should be for everyone, and nobody should be afraid to enjoy the things that make them happy.

I'm also pretty sure that playing a campaign with the Indestructibles would be a lot of fun, if somewhat chaotic.

I hope you enjoy this foray into superheroes playing a tabletop RPG—turns out it's a setting I'd like to revisit. I hope this isn't the last gaming session our intrepid heroes have together.

Matthew Phillion
Salem, Massachusetts
December 2017

Chapter 1: Roll for initiative

It all started with Entropy Emily, of course.

It'd been a quiet week for the Indestructibles. The quintet of young super-powered heroes had finally seen a lull in action. No monsters rising up out of the sewers, no super villains threatening the City. There had been some of the usual stuff, low-level crime to fight, a flooding situation in another state that needed their help in the rescue effort, but really, for a team that regularly encountered world-threatening trouble… things had been pretty low-key.

Which meant, of course, that they started bickering.

Solar-powered girl and team leader Jane "Solar" Hawkins was actively avoiding the ballerina-turned-vigilante Kate "Dancer" Miller over some argument about use of force. Kate was also miffed at Titus, the young werewolf whom nobody was allowed to call Kate's boyfriend despite evidence to the contrary, for reasons none of them could quite figure out. Gravity-controller and all around instigator Entropy Emily was in trouble with all three of them for drawing cartoons about their behavior, and now Billy "Straylight" Case, Emily's best friend, was annoyed at her for starting trouble and dragging him into it (even though, as Emily pointed out, it was Billy's idea to draw the cartoons in the first place). Even the alien inhabiting Billy's brain—the source of his superpowers—was in on the action, annoyed at all five of the teenagers for acting, well, like teenagers.

And to make matters worse, Emily had called some sort of "group meeting" in the control room, which no one wanted to attend, but everyone felt compelled to show up to anyway.

"You know she's not even going to show up herself," Billy said, his feet up, as always, on the table in the control center they used as their main conference space. The room was dominated by a large table that had, for more than one generation of heroes, been the place where battle plans were made and philosophical debates raged. Today, it was a staging area for an argument.

"I will too show up," Emily said, walking into the room with one of her signature bubbles of float drifting beside her, carrying a stout, colorful box. She waved the bubble of float above the table and let it drop. The box landed between her four teammates with a clunk.

Jane leaned over to check it out. The box was adorned with colorful fantasy art. Knights with swords, facing dragons and monsters, piles of treasure at their feet.

"What's this?" Jane asked.

"This, kiddos, is our team-building exercise," Emily said, plopping down in a chair at the end of the table.

"How about no," Billy said.

"You don't honestly think you can lead us in a team building exercise," Kate grumbled.

Titus, however, slid the box in front of him and popped the cover open.

"Where'd you get this?" he asked.

"Doc's study," Emily said.

"You... took something from Doc's study?" Jane said, actual worry in her voice. It wasn't so much that Doc Silence, the magician who acted as the group's mentor, would be angry that Emily had been in his study. Jane's concern was more based on the fact that, as a magician, a lot of things in Doc's rooms were legitimately dangerous, and some of the most dangerous things he had looked completely benign.

"It's a board game," Emily said. "I didn't steal the Necronomicon from his desk. Look at that. Tell me how it looks dangerous."

"It looks... fun," Titus said.

"See?" Emily said, beaming proudly. "I knew I could win at least one of you over."

"It looks like it's got a Dungeons and Dragons feel to it," Titus said, pulling out instructions from within the box. "Oh hey, character classes."

Kate stared at the werewolf, hard.

"It's legitimately alarming how excited you are about this," Kate said.

"I was a geek, Kate. I liked Dungeons and Dragons," Titus said. He turned his attention back to Emily. "But I do not think that playing a game in which Emily is the Dungeon Master, with ultimate power to manipulate and annoy the living hell out of all of us, is a good idea."

Emily gave Titus a vaudevillian wink.

"That's the best part. This is like Dungeons and Dragons, but instead of one of us being the Dungeon Master, we all play together. Against the game. There's rules so the game is the villain and we're the heroes."

Billy stood up.

"Okay, that's great. I'm out," Billy said.

Kate stood up too, and started to leave.

"Come on, guys," Jane said. Titus handed her a stack of cards with different types of characters they could play emblazoned on them. The artwork was luxurious and highly detailed. "She's right. We've been ready to get into a fist fight with each other all week. What's the harm in playing a game for a few hours? The world doesn't need rescuing at the moment."

"You're going to play a tabletop RPG?" Billy said.

"A what?" Jane said.

Emily slapped her hands down on the table.

"I knew it! I knew you knew all about these games! Billy Case, you will never be able to hide your inner geek!"

Billy sat back down, his face slightly red.

"Let me see the cards," Billy said. "Don't tell anybody about this."

"I'm already Tweeting about it," Emily said. "Straylight, the cockiest member of the Indestructibles, reveals his inner geek during a game of…"

"Don't," Billy said.

Kate looked the group over, sighed, and sat down next to Titus.

"Fine. I'll play along. For a little while," she said.

"Good," Emily said, rubbing her hands together and pulling pieces out of the box to create a game board. "First up, we should pick our character classes. Kate, I nominate you to play a monk."

Kate glared at her.

"What about me strikes you as someone who should play a religious person who has taken a vow of silence?" Kate said.

"Wrong kind of monk," Emily said. She picked up one of the cards Jane had set aside and handed it to Kate. There was a woman in loose-fitting clothes on the card, holding a staff, standing in a classic martial artist's pose. "Monks in this game are hand-to-hand experts. Like you. It'd be like you're playing yourself."

Kate looked at the card, wrinkled her nose, and then nodded, her body language uncharacteristically agreeable.

"Okay," she said, sounding almost pleased. "I can do that. That sounds fair."

"Who's this one, with the armor and the sword. She looks amazing," Jane said. She held up a card to show the rest of the table. Emily and Titus both laughed.

"Naturally," Titus said.

"You're going to need to translate the geek thing for me," Jane said. "I've clearly done something funny."

"That's a paladin," Emily said. "Like a holy knight. Lawful good. Ultimate nice guy. Always does the right thing. Saves puppies and kittens."

Jane smiled sheepishly.

"I walked right into that, didn't I," she said.

"There's worse things than always being a good person, Jane," Titus said, still smirking. He placed one of the cards down on the table. "Well, I found mine."

"A druid?" Kate said. "I'm going to assume there's some science fiction and fantasy trope I'm not privy to here."

Titus shrugged, clearly uncomfortable with his girlfriend-but-not learning about how much he knew of fantasy tabletop games.

"Druids are forest guardians who can usually—" Titus started saying, but Kate cut him off, reading from the card.

"A druid character can also transform into a dire wolf or bear at will," Kate read. "This is almost as funny as Jane playing the white knight thing."

"Paladin," Emily said.

"Whatever," Kate said. "I'm wondering if Titus can do any of these other things. Healing spells, manipulating plants. Are you holding out on us?"

"Yes," Titus said in a deadpan tone. "I am actually able to make trees get up and walk around. I just never did this during one of our missions because I have hay fever."

Billy held up the cover of the box and pointed to one of the characters, dressed in green, wielding a bow and arrow.

"I want to be Robin Hood," he said.

"Billy, stop pretending you don't know what that is," Emily said.

Billy locked eyes with her. Emily stared back. The test of wills was palpable.

"Fine!" Billy said. "I like playing rangers. Is there a ranger in that pile of cards?"

"I love that we're learning the depths of Billy's inner geek," Emily said. Jane slid one of the cards across the table. Billy caught it.

"Cool," Billy said. "And what exactly are you going to play, Emily? I can't imagine there's a snarky character class that specializes in bubbles of float in that pile."

"I am clearly a multi-class rogue/fighter/mage specializing in Transmutation," Emily said.

Everyone went quiet at that. Finally, Titus spoke.

"Wow," Titus said. "Just... wow."

"Fine," Emily said. "I'm a bard."

"Of course you are," Billy said.

"I don't get it," Jane said.

"Me either," Kate said.

Titus just shook his head.

"Just... just roll with it," Titus said. "It requires too much explanation."

The team pulled their chairs in closer around the map as Emily doled out cards with things like swords and spells on them. The box contained surprisingly detailed figurines of each of the characters they'd decided to play, which she arranged in a starting area on the map. She flipped open the instructions.

"Okay, so here's the deal," Emily said. "We are a group of adventurers, and we're tasked with rescuing the land from different dangers."

"Dangers?" Jane said.

"Monsters and stuff," Emily said. "We work our way across the map until we have to face an evil sorcerer who is holding the entire kingdom captive."

"Don't we get enough rescuing in our real lives?" Billy said. "I mean, clearly I've outed myself as a D&D guy, but… This feels like we're playing our special version of 'Life.'"

"But you have a magic bow and a sword, Billy," Emily said.

"Good point. Okay. So what do we do first?" Billy said.

"Well, like any good role playing game, I think we're supposed to roll for initiative to see who goes first," Emily said.

Titus scooped up the dice inside the box and handed them to Kate.

"Want to do the honors?" Titus said.

Kate accepted the dice and shrugged.

"I guess if we're really doing this, I might as well try to enjoy it," she said.

"Good," Titus said.

Kate shook a pair of dice in her hand—almost smiling, Jane noticed, a rare sight on the vigilante's face—and let the dice roll across the map.

And then the entire room lit up, went entirely silent...

And the Indestructibles were gone.

Chapter 2: It always begins with a tavern

One minute they were safe and warm around their table, and the next, they stood in the middle of a dark forest, a light rain falling onto their shoulders.

"I'm going to give you the benefit of the doubt," Billy said, directing his words at Emily and Emily alone, "...that you didn't know this was going to happen."

Given Emily's predilection to pranks, Billy thought, I'm being pretty generous here, right Dude?

Dude, Billy's symbiotic alien companion and sometimes conscience, didn't answer. Probably pouting, Billy thought.

"I had no idea this was going to happen," Emily said, looking up into the sky, then at the group. "You guys really need to see how you're all dressed."

Billy looked down at himself. He wore shades of green and brown, with a leather vest studded with flat metal circles. He had a green hood resting on his shoulders that he pulled over his head to deflect the rain. As he did, his sleeve got caught on the end of an elaborate longbow strapped to his back.

"I have a bow and arrow--and what are *you* wearing, Em?" he said.

Emily, the perennial victim of her own fashion sense, looked like something out of an Alice and Wonderland drawing. She had mismatched leggings, black and white striped up one leg and green and black striped down the other, with slouching, oversized boots on her feet. She had a loose-fitting shirt, gleamingly blue, to match her hair, which had remained her usual day-glow blue as well. She wore a short sword at her waist and had a lute strapped to her back. Also...

"Emily, what's wrong with your ears?" Jane said.

Emily reached up and touched her ears, which were now far too big, with long, pointed tips.

"I'm an elf!" she said, jumping off the ground repeatedly. "I'm an elf! I always wanted to be an elf!"

"Like, do we need to give you a sock or something to grant your freedom?" Billy said.

Emily started laughing.

"Don't make fun til you check yourself out, Legolas," Emily said. Billy grabbed his ears. They had remained normal sized, but both ended in slight points, like Spock from Star Trek.

"No, no no no," Billy said, then caught sight of Kate standing in the rain, looking more miserable than usual. "This is... Why is Kate dressed like Rey from 'Star Wars?'"

Kate's standard non-fighting wardrobe of athletic-wear had been replaced with brown pants, cut off mid-calf, and a lighter top that wrapped around her torso like a robe. Her arms were encased in gray bandages from knuckle to bicep. She had a long staff slung across her back.

"I was really hoping this was some sort of hallucination," Kate said. She sounded more disappointed than enraged. "Titus, tell me that thing on your head isn't what it looks like."

Titus was dressed in ragged leather, with a long, green cloak draped over his shoulders. He held a spear in one hand and had a curved sword hanging from his belt. The highlight of his bizarre ensemble, though, was a taxidermied wolf's head, which he wore like a cap. He tore it off his head and almost flung it away in disgust.

"Gah! No! It's like I'm wearing one of my relatives as a hat! This is horrible!"

"Um, guys?" Jane said. In unison, Billy, Emily, Kate, and Titus turned their attention to the solar-powered girl.

"You even do group hallucinations better than the rest of us," Emily said.

Jane wore golden armor, a glamorous combination of plate and chain, a red cloak pinned to one shoulder. She had a long sword at her hip, a shield on her back, and a winged helmet tucked under one arm.

"Just once, I'd like to do something as well as you do," Billy said.

Kate adjusted the staff on her back and pushed rain-slicked hair out of her face. She poked Titus in the arm, hard.

"Ow," he said, glaring at her. "What was that for?"

"Testing," Kate said. She poked him again. Titus backed away, grimacing. "I don't think this is a hallucination. I think this is real."

"We're really in the game," Billy said.

"It all feels real," Jane said. "Everything sounds real, the rain, the wind in the trees. This armor isn't exactly light."

"So we should assume this isn't some kind of dream," Kate said. She turned to Emily. "You took that game from Doc's study."

"Oh, don't go blaming this on me," Emily said.

"I don't see how this isn't entirely your fault," Titus said.

"How was I supposed to know the game was like cursed or something?" Emily said.

"You took literally took it from a wizard!" Billy said. "How could you not know it was cursed or something!"

Emily pointed at each of her colleagues in turn.

"All of you agreed to play it," Emily said. "I didn't claim I picked it up at Toys R Us."

Jane sighed, adjusting her armor absently, as if she'd been trained to wear medieval chainmail.

"We have to assume there's a way out, then," Jane said. "Standing around in the rain isn't going to fix anything. Where do we go first?"

Titus pointed to the east with his spear. In the distance, not far away, they could see a building, with a welcoming red roof, smoke drifting pleasantly from two chimneys.

"A tavern," Emily said. "Of course there's a tavern. It always begins with a tavern."

"Well then," Jane said. "I guess we know our first stop."

Chapter 3: You look like a hearty band of adventurers

Jane noticed, with some discomfort, that distance didn't seem to work normally in this place, wherever they were.

"We got here way too fast," she said as they walked up the stony path toward the tavern.

Billy looked over his shoulder toward where they started.

"Did we just walk like two miles in ten minutes?"

Titus hung his wolf's head hat on a sign at the foot of the steps, started to walk away, then went back and picked it back up again.

"What," Kate said, questioning him.

"I don't know what to do with it," he said. "I'm grossed out, but it also feels really disrespectful to throw it away."

"You know it's probably not real," Kate said.

"I... I'm having some difficulty processing this," Titus said.

"None of us are really okay with being trapped in a fantasy world," Jane said. "It's okay."

"Oh no, I'm fine with that," Titus said. "I just don't know what I should do with the head of my ancestors. It's freaking me out."

Emily sidled up beside him, took the wolf's head hat, and opened up a satchel she had over her shoulder. She tucked the hat inside and closed the bag.

"Better?"

"Better," Titus said.

Jane climbed the front steps to the tavern and stopped.

"I... Have any of you ever been in a bar before?" she asked.

"I've been in, like, a Friday's," Billy said. "Does that count?"

"Close enough," Kate said, walking past everyone and into the bar. Jane and Billy looked at each other, shrugged, and followed her in.

The interior was dark, lit by a pair of massive fireplaces on either side of the room. Hand-crafted tables of varying sizes and shapes littered the hall-like room, and the occupants of those tables were as varied as the furniture. A group of dwarves straight out of Tolkien's books laughed raucously in the corner. A couple of lean, armed men spoke softly in a darkened booth. A group of minstrels, colorfully dressed but looking like they'd seen better days, played near the bar, singing a song about smoky hills and lost loves. Mud-caked farmers, a soot-covered blacksmith, a merchant in a fancy purple waistcoat... the room was filled to the brim with every high fantasy stereotype they could imagine.

Emily stopped dead in her tracks and clapped her hands giddily.

"I love this. I love this. Can we stay? This is amazing."

Billy, on the other hand, looked uncharacteristically self-conscious. He caught Jane's eye.

"Anyone else the least bit concerned about how we ended up on the set of the Hobbit and none of us is even slightly alarmed at this? We're taking this weirdly in stride."

"Or Strider, if we're making Tolkien jokes," Emily said.

"I wasn't making a joke," Billy said.

"You have an alien inside your brain and I'm a werewolf," Titus muttered. "I think we've just come to the point where weird is our new normal."

Emily grabbed Billy's hand and dragged him to the bar. Kate put a hand on Jane's armored shoulder.

"We are actually concerned about this, right? Because I'm worried," Kate said.

"Yeah," Jane said, nodding., "I'm worried too."

Before they could continue the conversation, though, Emily's voice cut shrilly through the din of the tavern.

"What do you mean you don't have butterbeer?" she said.

Titus, who had hung back with Kate at the doorway, started toward the bar as well.

"I'll go get her," he said, shaking his head. "I don't care if this is reality or a hallucination, Emily's going to get us killed if we don't rein her in."

Jane caught several stares from the patrons as she and Kate bellied up to the bar as well. Some, like the farmers, seemed worried. The musicians eyed the team curiously, but never stopped playing. One patron, a heavyset woman in a deep burgundy dress, watched them with an unwavering and unreadable look.

"We're drawing attention to ourselves," Jane whispered to Kate.

"Well, at least that's normal," Kate said. Beside them, Titus spoke in hushed tones to Emily, who answered back at full volume, with phrases like "immersive game play" and "suspension of disbelief" and "staying in-character." Jane sighed. The barmaid, a round-faced woman with a head full of curls almost as fiery red as Jane's own locks, gave her a sympathetic nod.

"There's one in every traveling group, isn't there," she said. Jane smiled back. Then she felt a hand on her elbow.

"Excuse me," a soft, strong voice said.

Jane turned quickly, startled. She sensed rather than saw Kate move to a protective position a few feet away, ready to fight. Titus and Emily stopped arguing instantly. We're still a good team, Jane thought, pride swelling in her chest at how the Indestructibles leapt to each other's defense. But in this case, it seemed unnecessary. The voice belonged to the woman in the burgundy dress, who stood in front of Jane, arms folded up inside a cloak just a shade darker than the rest of her outfit.

"I'm sorry to disturb you, sir knight," the woman said. Jane wrinkled her eyebrows, momentarily confused, before remembering she'd taken on the role of a paladin. She stood up straighter, trying, as Emily suggested, to get into character.

"That's okay," Jane said, trying to make her voice deeper, feeling more ridiculous with each passing second. "What can I do for you?"

"You seem like a hearty band of adventurers," the woman said. She had wispy gray hair bound up in tight curls, her nose a curt button of red in a pale face.

"We are! We are hearty adventurers. A band of them," Emily said. Billy rested a hand on Emily's shoulder, and she let her hand drop so that she "accidentally" punched him in the groin. Billy took his hand off Emily's shoulder and stepped back involuntarily.

"Well if that's the case, I'm glad I found you," the woman said. "Because our little village is in dire need of the help of adventurers such as yourself."

"Village?" Billy said. Jane knew what he was saying--they hadn't seen a village on their way, only the tavern. Where was this village?

"I…" Jane started to say, but faltered. Emily jumped in without hesitation.

"We're glad to offer our services," Emily said, her voice over-dramatic, with a hint of a bad impersonation of a British accent weaved in. "What can we do for this fair town?"

"There's a tribe of goblins in the hills," the woman said. "I'm the mayor of this town, and I've been authorized to hire a group such as yourself to drive them off. They're stealing our livestock and causing much trouble, but we don't have the fighters we need to scare them away."

"Goblins," Billy said. He opened his mouth to say something else, but just shook his head, and repeated: "Goblins."

Again, Jane started to talk, but Emily took the lead.

"Goblins are our specialty, ma'am," Emily said. "Just point us toward their camp, and we'll make sure they trouble you no more."

The old woman rattled off vague directions, involving "due west" and "over the bendy hill" and "near the burbling river." Jane barely followed, but Emily nodded as if she understood every word perfectly.

"I am so glad you're willing to help us," the old woman said. "We'll gladly furnish you with a reward when you return."

Emily held up her hands magnanimously.

"No reward is necessary," Emily said. "We're all about doing good deeds."

The old woman thanked them, shaking each of their hands, and then returned to a seat by the fire. Several of the farmers walked over to chat with her quietly.

"Goblins," Billy said again.

"She's an NPC!" Emily said.

"A what?" Kate said.

"A non-player character," Titus explained. "I think Emily might be right. If we're the players…"

"NPCs in games like this give you missions," Emily said. "They push the story forward."

A smile spread across Jane's face. It was starting to make sense.

"And we're the players. So, she's part of the game," Jane said.

Kate sighed, the sound falling somewhere between relief and frustration.

"We're literally in the game," Kate said. "So we have to… beat the game to escape?"

"I don't know," Emily said. She picked up a cup of something from the bar and took a long, enthusiastic sip, grimaced, and set it back down.

"What was that," Jane said.

"I think it was goat's milk," Emily said, her nose wrinkling. "I hope that's what it was. I hope it was goat's milk. You know what? I don't actually want to know what it was. Anyway—I say we try to play along. Maybe Kate's right and we just have to beat the game to get back to the real world."

"By fighting… goblins," Billy said.

"Could be worse, Billy," Titus said. "She could have told us there was a dragon in the hills instead."

Chapter 4: Flight is not an option

They left the tavern with a hand-drawn map showing them the way to the goblin cave, playing their roles as they waved goodbye to the goodly little mayor. As soon as they turned a corner on the muddy road, out of sight of the little inn, Billy took off at a run, leapt into the air, and landed face-first in the grime.

Emily watched this happen without batting an eye.

"I'm assuming you did that for a reason, champ," she said.

Billy pulled himself up out of the mud, wiping his face. Behind him, an owl hooted. Jane offered him a hand, which he accepted. She pulled him to his feet.

"I was checking to see if my powers worked," Billy said.

"So flight's off the list," Emily said.

"Yeah," Billy said. He nodded at Jane. "You?"

Jane shook her head.

"I'm not going to give it a test run like you just did, but I don't think I can fly here," she said. "I'm working with the assumption that flight is not an option."

"Your hair is normal, too," Emily said.

"Which is just as well, if we're trying to not attract attention," Kate said softly. "Should we assume you're not impervious to harm now?"

Jane shrugged.

"Again, I'd rather not give it a test run, but let's assume I'm not," Jane said.

"I haven't heard Dude for hours," Billy said. "I don't feel cut off from him. Like, I can still feel him creeping around the corners of my mind, but I can't hear him."

The owl hooted again. Billy looked up and around, giving the bird a dirty look.

"So your powers aren't gone, they're just… suppressed," Titus said, leaning on the spear he'd appeared with in this fictional world.

"What about you?" Kate asked.

"I can still transform if we need me to," Titus said.

"How do you you—" Billy started to say.

"Trust me, I can," Titus said sharply.

"But—" Billy said again.

Titus waved him off.

"You don't want to know," Titus said.

"Yes, we do," Kate said.

Titus's shoulders slumped.

"If you can feel Dude creeping around in the corners of your mind, the wolf inside me is breathing heavily into my ear," Titus said.

"That is one of the most disturbing things you've ever said," Emily said.

The owl hooted a third time. Billy shook his head, exasperated.

"Hey, at least we know one of us still has our powers, and seriously, is anyone else hearing an owl insult you?" Billy said. "Like, it's not in real words. I can just tell he's insulting me in bird."

The entire group stared at him for a long moment.

"I have no idea what you're talking about, Billy," Jane said.

The owl hooted again and Billy swung around and shot the bird an obscene gesture.

"Well so are you!" Billy yelled.

"And... he's lost it," Emily said.

Billy stomped his foot, splashing more mud back up his pant leg. Jane and Kate both took an involuntary step back to avoid the runoff.

"So not only can I no longer fly, this game we're trapped in has given me the ability to understand the language of avian insults," Billy said. He yelled up at the sky. "Stop yelling at me, you bossy, judgmental, feathered—Dude?"

"Billy, why don't you sit down," Jane said.

He didn't. Instead, he held out his hand, and an elegant silver-and-brown owl drifted down from the treetops and landed on his wrist. The owl hooted at all of them. Billy laughed.

"I can't make out his real words, but I can understand that really upset that he's stuck inside an owl," Billy said.

Emily jumped up and down, her heavy costume boots spraying mud everywhere.

"You're a ranger! You have an animal companion!" Emily said.

The owl hooted again. It sounded distinctly indignant.

"That is definitely bird-talk for saying he's not happy about being an animal companion," Billy said.

"I think we picked up on that," Titus said. "Good to have you back, Dude."

The owl hooted once again, scurrying up Billy's arm to rest on his shoulder.

Jane laughed lightly, then waved at Emily to calm down.

"Any other tricks we should know about based on our, um, characters?" she said.

"Well for starters," Emily said, "Why don't you try pulling your sword from its scabbard."

Jane raised an eyebrow, then reached to her belt and drew her sword.

Flames instantly appeared along the blade, dancing and twitching brightly. The rain sizzled as it spattered against it. Jane turned the blade over, back and forth in her hand, and then held it aloft.

Despite it all, despite being scared and worried for her friends, and far from home, and trapped wherever this place was, Jane couldn't help it. She couldn't fight back the smile.

"I don't get it," Jane said.

"That's your flaming sword, Sir Jane," Emily said.

"I love it," Jane said.

"I told you guys you'd like this game," Emily said, grinning like a madwoman.

Chapter 5: Here there be goblins

"I'm going to regret asking this," Kate said. "But what are those?"

The team lay on their bellies on a ridge overlooking a shallow valley so that only their eyes and the tops of their heads peered over. Below them, dozens of small, homely creatures puttered about, green-skinned and misshapen, with heads too big for their scrawny bodies. The creatures bickered, and occasionally broke out into fistfights with each other, chattering away in a mishmash of familiar words and another language that sounds like gibberish spoken at a high speed.

"Those," Emily said solemnly, "Are goblins."

"These are the monsters hounding the village?" Billy said. "They look like hairless squirrels."

"They look like they can't stop fighting each other long enough to bother anyone else," Jane said. "We're not really supposed to exterminate them, are we?"

"That was kind of the implication of the quest," Emily said.

"I feel like this is an unfair fight," Jane said.

"You say that now," Titus said, taking a headcount. "But if they swarm us you might regret that statement."

"Y'know, in most games like this…" Emily began.

"We are not in a game," Kate said.

"In most games like this," Emily repeated, emphasizing "game" tauntingly, "There's sometimes a non-violent solution. Maybe we just need to figure out the non-violent solution."

Just as she said this, one goblin stabbed another goblin in the chest. The other goblin yanked the knife out and used it to stab the first goblin back. They both keeled over on the ground, probably dying.

"Or we're going to have to kill the little sociopaths," Emily said.

"We don't kill," Jane said.

"On purpose," Titus muttered.

"What?" Jane said.

"What Titus is saying is he's probably, probably killed people before," Billy said. "When he's all wolfed out and stuff."

"Thanks, Billy," Titus said. "I really needed the reminder."

"I'm here to help," Billy said.

"Okay, so here's the plan," Jane said.

"Jane," Kate interrupted.

"Can I at least suggest my plan before you undermine it?" Jane said.

"Jane, we may not have enough time for me to undermine your plan," Kate said. "Look."

Down below, one of the goblins was looking right at them with huge, yellow eyes. While his peers fought and screeched around him, this one goblin stood completely still. Watching.

"Oh, come on," Billy said.

"He sees us," Titus said.

"Maybe he's just glitching out," Emily said. "I bet he's just staring into space."

Then the staring goblin started yelling and jumping up and down, pointing to the top of the hill where the Indestructibles hid.

"He saw us," Billy said.

"I guess we're about to commit genocide," Jane said, her voice exhausted. She stood up and unsheathed her sword, which burst into flames along the blade. Kate unslung her staff from her shoulder. Billy nocked an arrow with his bow.

Emily pulled out a lyre.

"Oh, come on!" Billy said.

"What are you doing," Kate said. She looked at Titus. "What is she doing?"

"I'm the bard," Emily said. "I'm going to play you inspirational battle music."

Billy looked down the hill.

"Guys, there's about forty goblins running right at us on stumpy little green legs," Billy said.

Emily strummed her lyre dramatically.

"Ahem," Emily said.

"You're not going to help us fight?" Jane said, sliding her shield onto her forearm.

"I'm the bard," Emily said again, as if that explained everything.

"Oh for… Never mind, guys, I've got this," Titus said, giving up. He left the group behind and charged down the hill, swiftly transforming into his werewolf form—only here in this fantasy land, that form was even more monstrous than back home. His body was more beastly, his shoulders ridiculously broad; his wolfish head looked less like a true incarnation of a wolf and more something out of a child's nightmare.

"Dammit," Kate said, preparing to race after him. "We can't let him do this on his own."

"Wait," Jane said. She pointed down the hill with her sword.

The goblins had all stopped charging. Instead, most stood in awe, their oversized eyes enormous with a combination of fear and worship. A few even dropped to the ground, prostrate.

"What are they doing?" Jane said.

"Oh!" Emily said.

"'Oh' does not explain what's going on, Em," Billy said.

"In a lot of fantasy games, goblins worship wolf gods," Emily said. "I think they…"

"They think Titus is a god?" Billy said.

"He just totally Threepio-ed them," Emily said.

Even Titus looked confused by the situation—he'd stopped his aggressive charge down the hill and now stood, bewildered, as the little goblins looked up at him adoringly. One even ran over to hug his leg. Jane could tell it was all Titus could do to not shake him off like a bug.

"Well," Jane said. "Now I really don't know what to do."

"I do," Emily said.

"Of course you do," Kate said, but before anyone could stop her, Emily began traipsing down the hillside, strumming her lyre.

"Behold! I am the minstrel of the Wolf God! Look upon him with wonder, little goblins, for the Wolf God loves you! He is here to answer your prayers!"

"She's going to get us all killed," Kate said.

"Or not," Billy said. "Look."

The goblins began to follow Emily like a procession, and gasped as one when she put a protective hand on Titus's furry shoulder.

The crowd of goblins parted and an elderly female staggered forward, leaning heavily on a cane. She looked like debris washed up by the sea and left in the sun to dry.

"You help us?" the elder goblin asked.

Emily looked up the hill at Jane. Jane nodded—keep going.

"Of course! What else would the benevolent Wolf God be here to do?" she said.

"Come," the elder goblin said. "Sit. We have rat stew. We share and tell you of our troubles."

"Rat stew," Emily said, smiling uncomfortably. "Mm, my favorite. Lead on!"

Chapter 6: There's always a bigger monster

Billy stared at the cup of rat stew in his hands and tried very cautiously to find a way to throw it into the nearby bushes. Times like these he wished Dude was still in his head and not an owl perched on his shoulder so he'd have someone to complain with.

"Just eat it," Emily said.

"No," Billy said.

"We're in a game. You're not really eating rat. You're eating imaginary rat."

"I don't want to know what imaginary rat tastes like," Billy said.

"Fine," Emily said. "Give me yours."

He did, and Emily tossed the cup back with a dramatic gesture. The goblins sitting around the fire with them all nodded their gigantic heads in approval.

"I'm winning over the natives, Billy Case. Watch and learn," Emily said.

Meanwhile, Titus was still in werewolf form, and he'd lost all dignity. Little goblin children were weaving flowers into his fur clumsily. The goblin chieftain offered to slaughter a goat for him to eat, but Jane, ever the diplomat, explained that the Wolf God was not hungry right now, but thank you.

Oddly enough, Kate seemed to be the most effective communicator with the little green creatures. She chatted with the tribe's shaman and chief, drawing maps in the dirt.

"You'd think someone with such a short fuse would be bad at this part," Billy said.

"They use short words, she uses short sentences," Emily said. "It's a natural fit."

As if on cue, Kate gestured for them all to gather around and listen.

"They say they're running from something," Kate said. "And they're generally scared of humans, so for them to run toward the village means whatever they're running from must be scarier than we are."

"Great," Billy said.

"There's always a bigger monster," Emily said.

"So we, what, go slay the monster that the goblins are afraid of so they can move backward and stay away from the humans?" Jane said.

"I don't remember this part of Lord of the Rings," Billy said.

The shaman, the elderly female who had stopped the scene when Titus transformed, chattered and pointed at something Kate had drawn in the dirt.

"I hear words I'm supposed to understand in there, but I'm not understanding them," Jane said. "Is it me or is she speaking really quickly?"

"Quickly and at a pitch not unlike someone who had just inhaled helium," Billy said.

Kate exhaled angrily.

"If you could be quiet for five minutes, I could find out where the monster that chased her tribe away is," Kate said.

The female goblin chattered away again. Kate's face dropped.

"I got that one," Billy said.

"Did she just correct you and say monsters, plural?" Jane said.

"Monsters, plural," Kate said. She looked at Emily with complete seriousness. "I am so mad at you for getting us stuck here."

"Be mad at me later. Get location of monsters first," Emily said.

The chieftain weighed in next. His voice was deeper, but somehow even less intelligible, a deep rumble that sounded like a frog trying to cough up a hairball.

"Yep, nope, I didn't get that one," Billy said.

"He said we have to go up over that ridge, then down into a..." Kate said. The turned to Jane.

"What," Jane said.

"I'm trying to figure out if he said..." Kate said.

"Cave, he definitely said cave," Emily said.

"I hate caves," Jane said.

"I know," Kate said. "I had a feeling you wouldn't be happy about this."

"Guys, we're basically trapped in a Dungeons and—" Emily started.

"Don't say it," Billy said.

"But you didn't expect a dungeon crawl?" Emily said.

Titus let out a small whine. Billy saw a tiny goblin child fall asleep on the werewolf's foot. Titus's face might still have been in monstrous form, but he looked at Billy with a comically human expression, begging for help.

"I think Titus might be the only one who's totally okay with us going into a dungeon," Billy said.

Emily hopped up and strummed her lyre. The goblin tribe took notice.

"New friends!" Emily said in what Billy had come to recognize as her trying-to-sound-British-but-more-like-Ren-Faire voice. "We will defeat this monster for you!"

"Monsters," Billy corrected. "Plural."

"We will defeat these monsters for you!" Emily said, editing herself. "You will have your homes back soon!"

"Or we'll be eaten by whatever monsters are waiting for us," Jane said. "What were the monsters like, anyway?"

Jane pantomimed with the goblin leaders, asking for details. The shaman mimicked a sort of shuffling gait, slow and creepy.

"Tell me she didn't just do charades to tell us we're fighting zombies," Billy said.

"It'll be fine," Emily said. "We're heroes, right?"

"I've decided the one upside to this is we all know exactly whose fault this is," Billy said.

Chapter 7: Dungeon crawl

"That," Jane said, the disappointment in her voice palpable. "That is definitely a cave."

They'd crossed the landscape—stereotypically green, with rough-hewn rocky outcroppings and tall trees, as if someone went to central casting and asked for a very ordinary medieval setting—and found the cave the goblin tribe had fled with disconcerting ease. Emily thought it was just part of the game they were trapped in, that the game would guide them where they needed to go to keep the story progressing. Kate thought something more sinister was at play.

Everyone else was simply more concerned about going into a cave.

"Nothing good ever happens in a cave," Titus said. "Every story. Every movie. Every book. Know what happens in caves? Bad things."

"Stop being melodramatic," Emily said.

"You really need to stop sounding like you're enjoying this," Titus said, pulling his cloak's hood down over his face as a light rain began to fall.

"This is part of the game! This is the best part of the game. The dungeon crawl. When a merry band of brave adventurers head into the darkness below to save the day."

"Look," Jane said. "We just have to do it. We want to go home, right?"

"No," Emily said.

"Yes," everyone said in unison.

"Then we go into the cave," Jane said.

"Dungeon," Emily corrected.

Jane ignored her and walked bravely and without pause down the slope toward the cave. Everyone else raced clumsily to catch up.

Kate sidled up next to Jane so they walked side by side.

"What's our play," Kate said.

"Kill the monster."

"Monsters," Kate corrected. "We don't even know what kind of monsters we're looking at."

"Could they be any worse than anything we fought in the real world?" Jane said.

Kate nodded.

"Fair point. Still," Kate said. "It feels like anything goes here. And we're not ourselves. None of you have the same powers you're used to."

Jane smiled at Kate.

"But we have you," Jane said. "And you're the same here as you are back home."

"Powerless and bitter?"

"Relentless and reliable," Jane said. "So if you have any ideas…"

They paused in front of the mouth of the cave. Kate exhaled.

"This is all her fault for getting us to try to socialize," Kate said.

"I heard that," Emily said.

Kate ignored her, instead walking into the cave, and the darkness beyond.

Chapter 8: The skeletons always move

"I always suspected I was claustrophobic, but I can now verify that I am," Billy said. Dude hooted on his shoulder. "Dude's claustrophobic too."

"Dude spends his entire life trapped in your brain," Emily said. "I'd get claustrophobic too."

I think I have a valid complaint, Billy thought. They'd made their way without incident deep into the cavern, following a long, narrow pathway down into the darkness. Someone had taken the time to light torches. Titus pointed out that if someone lit torches, that meant they weren't alone, but Emily assured them that unexplained lit torches were just part of the genre. Billy found that to be an unacceptable level of suspension of disbelief.

"You guys can believe the torches are just here, but I'm telling you, when the zombie ogre vampires come bubbling up out of the pits of hell..." he said.

Titus had called up some magical globe of light with a spell which floated beside the group, casting strange shadows on the wall. They all had their weapons drawn, and Jane's flaming sword also helped illuminate the dark hallways. Billy found himself longing for the halo of light Dude's powers always gave off.

If there was one bright side to the journey, it was that the tunnel never split—it went straight down, not giving them the option of getting lost. Finally, the corridor opened up into a large hall. This area had clearly been carved with deliberate care, with squared off walls and a more door-like archway to enter through. Long tables and benches indicated that this was once a dining area, though judging by the skeletons left sitting around some of those tables, it had not been used on a long time.

"They look like they're starving," Billy said.

"Dead guys," Titus said. "Awesome."

The dining hall had a door on each of its four walls, including the tunnel they'd just emerged from. The doorway on the left was buried in rubble from a long-ago cave-in. The other looked passable.

"Two doors," Jane said. "Do we split up?"

"Never split the party," Emily said.

"We could cover more ground," Jane said.

"First rule of these games. Never split the party," Emily said. "Haven't you ever listened to Acquisitions, Inc.?"

"We split the party all the time in the real world," Jane said. "I don't get it."

"It's just..." Emily said, her voice rising with anxiety. "It's always a bad idea to split the party. That's how someone ends up getting eaten by a floating eyeball or falls into a pit of acid or absorbed by a cube of evil jelly."

"You play these games for fun?" Kate asked.

"Anyway," Jane said. "Two doorways. If we're not allowed to, um, split the party..."

"The one on the far wall," Titus said.

Kate sighed heavily.

"This really is the least attractive thing about you," Kate said.

"You can smell which... you can tell which corridor the monsters are down by scent?" Jane said.

"If you only knew how this superpower has negatively impacted my life you would never look at me the same way," Titus said.

Jane jumped a little as Billy put a hand on her shoulder.

"Guys," Billy said.

"Far wall it is," Jane said. "What, Billy."

"Guys," Billy repeated.

"What," Jane said again.

"Guys, the skeletons are moving," Billy said.

"No," Kate said. "No, we are not dealing with skeletons that come back to life. We're not."

"Oh man," Emily said "The skeletons always move. I should've thought of that."

"The skeletons always move?" Kate said. "Always? You play this game for fun!"

Titus unslung the long spear from his shoulder as Jane adjusted her grip on her flaming sword.

"I suppose now's a good time to mention how much Kate hates horror movies," Titus said.

"The real world is terrifying enough I don't see the point in voluntarily watching horror for fun," Kate said. "Or playing games with moving skeletons."

The skeletons, nearly a dozen in total, were all standing now, lifting rusted weapons with bony hands, trudging slowly, relentlessly, toward the group.

"Oh, the heck with this," Billy said. He let loose one of his arrows. The arrow, turned to light as it flew, illuminating the entire room. It struck the skeleton in the ribcage, blowing the creature apart, scattering its bones in every direction.

"What was that!" Titus said.

"I love this bow!" Billy said.

The skeletons closed in on them. Jane ran forward, swinging her flaming sword, knocking the head off one of the creatures. Kate joined her quickly, spinning her staff like a whirlwind. She knocked the legs out from one of the creatures and the head off another, though even headless, the body continued to reach for her. She smashed it again, this time connecting with the spine, and the skeletal creature crumbled.

Titus cast a spell that sent a searing golden light through two of the skeletons, turning them both to dust. Kate looked at him, bewildered.

"Spells against undead—y'know what, you're not interested in me explaining this to you," Titus said, knocking a skeleton to the ground with his spear.

"Not even remotely," Kate said, leaping into the air and smashing the butt of her staff down on Titus's skeleton, breaking its skull like an egg. "Just pretend I already know."

"Got it," Titus said, casting the spell again to destroy another skeleton.

Jane knocked two skeletons back with her shield, destroying one with her sword while Billy launched an arrow through the other. The looked at each other, and both were surprised to see the other smiling.

"This shouldn't be fun," Jane said. "We're fighting walking skeletons!"

"This is so much fun!" Billy said.

Then a bony hand landed on Billy's arm, and he was face to face with a rotting skull.

"Not fun! Not fun!" Billy said.

The skull went flying, replaced by the grim visage of Kate in battle mode. She finished off the skeleton's body with another sweep of her staff.

"Um. Thanks," Billy said.

Kate grunted at him and turned her attention to the rest of the battle. The skeletons lay crumbled in pieces across the dining hall. One skeletal hand twitched, but Jane stomped on it with her booted foot and the claw-like hand went still.

"Good job, guys," Emily said. She stood on one of the tables, lyre in hand, not a speck of battle dirt or skeleton dust on her.

"You didn't help at all, did you," Titus said.

"I'm the bard," Emily said, as if that explained everything.

"I can't believe you people do this for fun," Kate said, stomping away and into the next tunnel.

Chapter 9: Why does it have to be spiders

The torches grew fewer and the tunnels grew colder as they traveled deeper into the dungeon. The darkness became oppressive, though the walls seemed to give off a faint bluish light from a thin moss growing on the stone.

Another noticeable shift the further they went: cobwebs.

"Tell me," Jane said, frustration rising in her voice. "Tell me the cobwebs are just for visual effect."

"I'm sure they're just decorative," Emily said unconvincingly.

"Emily, I swear if there are spiders all over these caves," Jane said.

"Jane, if there are spiders big enough to leave webs this big behind, aesthetics are going to be the least of our concerns," Billy said.

"Shelob," Titus said.

"What's that?" Kate said.

"Don't you dare," Emily said.

"'Lord of the Rings.' Shelob. The giant spider that tries to eat Frodo," Titus said.

"Hush now, furball," Emily said. "Don't get everyone worked up."

"And the giant spiders that attack the company in the 'Hobbit,'" Titus said.

"So what you're saying is, there's a high probability we're going to encounter giant, homicidal spiders any minute now," Billy said.

"Why does it have to be spiders," Jane said.

"You're invulnerable and can shoot fire from your hands, but you're afraid of spiders?" Billy said.

Jane shot him a stern look.

"There's a difference between afraid and repulsed," Jane said.

"Spiders are cute!" Emily said.

"Does that mean giant spiders are extra cute?" Billy said.

"Spiders have too many eyes and legs and it kicks off my anxiety," Jane said.

"Guys," Kate said.

As always, a single word from Kate hushed the entire team. All conversation stopped. Jane strode over to Kate's side.

"You hear that?" Kate said.

"Nope," Emily said.

"Oh, I do," Titus said. He looked around the tight corridor anxiously. "I can't risk wolfing out in here. Too small a space. Don't want to chance hurting any of you."

"What. Wait. Why are you wolfing out?" Billy said. Then his mouth dropped open. "Oh that sounds like a lot of little feet running our way."

And then a spider the size of a golden retriever dropped from the ceiling and onto Billy's back.

"Ah! Get it off! Get it off!" he screamed. Dude hooted indignantly and flapped his wings defensively. Emily bashed the spider with her lyre, knocking the creature across the cavern floor. Billy drew a short sword from his belt and plunged it into the spider's carapace, spilling yellowy guts everywhere.

"Emily, I am going to kill you when we get home," Jane said, her voice pinched with what was either massive anxiety or rising vomit.

"Titus, can you tell which way they're coming?" Kate asked.

Titus started pointed back the way they came.

"Great," Kate said. "So we go deeper. Let's move."

The group broke into a run, Billy whining about the spider guts all over his clothes the whole way. They reached a fork in the tunnel and, unhesitatingly, Titus guided them left. As they ran, the sounds of spider-legs grew quieter, but the tunnel opened up, with more webbing, thicker and gray with age, gathered along the walls and ceiling.

"Titus…" Kate said.

"So… I'm just going to go out on a limb and say I think we were being herded," Titus said.

"Good job, champ," Billy said.

The corridor came to an end, terminating in a massive cave. Light filtered down from a break in the ceiling where daylight found its way in. Webs swayed in the breeze from that opening.

"I wonder if that's how they get up into the surface world to hunt," Emily said.

"Really. That's what you're wondering about right now," Billy said.

Dangling from the cave's ceiling were spindles of webs, ending in bulbous lumps. These, too, swayed lightly, stirred by the wind and the way they were weighted.

"What are those?" Titus said. He moved closer to one of them and reached out with his spear.

"Don't poke it!" Jane yelled. "What if it's eggs? Haven't you ever seen any horror movies? Don't poke spider eggs!"

"They're not eggs," Kate said. She pointed.

"Oh no," Jane said.

"They're little goblin pot stickers," Emily said.

Inside the webbed pod was a very dead goblin, staring back at them with vacant, dried yellow eyes.

"Yup, these are filled with dead goblins," Jane said, examining another. "We just walked into the pantry."

"Good job, Titus," Billy said.

"You guys asked me which way to run! I'm a werewolf, not a psychic!"

"Um," Kate said.

"Oh, what now," Billy said.

"That one's fresh," Kate said, pointing at one of the pods, which jiggled and swayed as if something inside were still struggling to escape.

Everyone looked at each other. Titus sighed.

"I got it," Titus said, walking up to the pod and slitting it open a few inches toward the bottom.

Inside, a terrified human face looked at them with wild eyes.

"Help! Help me!" the face said.

"Not dead!" Titus yelled, dropping the knife and taking a step back.

The man inside the pod had dark hair and a full beard, spider webs clinging to skin and hair. He continued to struggle as he talked.

"You've got to get me out of here, please, please help," he said.

"This has to be part of the game," Emily said.

"Game!" the man said. "You're in the game too? Oh, that's such a relief, please, help me out of…"

The man stopped talking as he looked past the group, his eyes growing impossibly wide.

"I'm not going to be happy when I turn around to see what you're looking at, am I," Titus said. He pivoted on his heel. "Nope, I'm not happy."

Emerging from the deeper shadows of the cavern, a spider the size of a station wagon crept toward them. It stepped with exaggerated grace on spindly legs, eyes like huge, reddish soap bubbles looking at them with ancient boredom. Its curved fangs dripped with greenish poison that hissed when it hit the ground.

"Don't let it bite you, it's p-p-p-par…" the man in the cocoon said.

"Poison, yeah, figured that one out on our own," Billy said.

"P-paralytic!" the man yelled.

"Awesome! Who doesn't love a little paralytic poison with breakfast," Billy said, drawing back his bow.

"We are never doing group bonding activities again," Kate said.

"You guys can't tell me this isn't at least a little fun," Emily said.

"Not real, right? Not real? Just a game," Jane said.

"Just a game," Emily said unconvincingly. "It's all pretend. Totally, completely, one hundred percent pretend."

"So what's the plan? On three?" Titus said, pulling his cloak back to prepare to transform.

And then Jane let loose a battle cry and ran forward, flaming sword in hand.

"Well, that's one way of doing it," Billy said.

The spider seemed almost startled by the aggression, rocking back on its tall legs as Jane ran. Jane swung her burning sword. The blade cut one of the spider's legs out from under it, and the creature squealed in rage. It snapped at Jane with its huge fangs, but Jane's burning sword cut into the right fang, snapping it in a spray of poison and spider guts. She slammed the spider's face with her shield then ducked underneath, raking the sword across the spider's undercarriage.

The creature clearly knew know how badly the battle was lost. It staggered away, leaving a trail of mucus-like blood behind, disappearing into the shadows. Jane started to run after the creature, but stopped and looked back at her friends. Slimy goop covered her armor. She smiled crazily at her friends.

"Not that's what I call overcoming a phobia!" Emily yelled.

Titus went back to cutting the stranger out of the cocoon. He looked thin and drawn, as if he'd been hungry a very long time.

"Thanks," he said. "My name is Eric. I can't tell you how happy I am to see other actual people here."

Titus helped him to his feet. Eric wobbled a little.

"Sorry," he said. "I've been upside-down for a while."

"How long have you been here?" Kate asked.

The man's expression went blank, and then took on a sour look.

"No idea. Months? Years? Time moves differently here," he said.

"You've been alone this whole time?" Titus said. Eric shook his head.

"I had companions. They... didn't make it."

"What do you mean, didn't make it," Billy said.

"They were killed," Eric said. "One got scooped up by a harpy. Another was crushed by an ogre. Then there was the wandering dragon..."

"Wait. What happens if you..." Jane said, joining them with a dazed look on her face.

"If you die here? You die in the real world," Eric said.

"Great, so we're in the Matrix, World of Warcraft edition," Billy said.

Jane went extremely pale, her skin taking on an almost greenish pallor.

"So without my powers, I could've..."

"Oh, I'm sure you were always perfectly safe," Emily said.

"Yeah, you totally could've just been eaten by a giant spider," Billy said.

Jane put her hands on Emily's shoulders and looked her dead in the eyes.

"You okay, Jane? You look terrible," Emily said.

"You are never in charge of game night ever again," Jane said.

And then she collapsed.

"Dude!" Emily yelled.

Kate dropped to her knees beside Jane to check her over.

"Pulse is steady," Kate said. "Oh."

"Oh?" Billy said.

Kate tilted the unconscious Jane's head sideways, revealing a thin scratch along her neck.

"Looks like some of the poison touched this cut," Kate said.

"Like I warned you," Eric said. "Paralytic."

"How long does it last?" Titus asked.

Eric frowned.

"From personal experience, I can tell you, if the spider doesn't bite you again, it starts to wear off in an hour or two."

"Awesome," Billy said. He slid one of Jane's arms over his shoulder and started to lift her. Emily took the other side. "So, provided we don't run into any more giant spiders…"

"She'll be awake when we get back to the surface," Kate said. "Enough talk. Let's get out of here before the mother spider decides to go for a second round."

Chapter 10: How to play the game

They returned to the goblin encampment, where small, green sociopaths greeted the returning heroes with much celebration, rat stew, and a drink made—if Kate's ability to translate had any accuracy—from distilled goat brains.

"But I may have got which organ incorrect," Kate explained as they sat around a camp fire, explaining the battle for the caverns and that the goblins were safe to return. "Or maybe the animal. It could be sheep brains, or maybe goat spleen."

"You're really selling us on this delightful beverage," Billy said, eyeing a measure of the grayish fluid in a cup Titus told him had probably once been a small animal skull.

The newcomer, Eric, drank it hungrily, making an awful face as he downed it.

"I'm sorry," he said sheepishly. "I haven't had food in days. I'll drink goat brain if I have to."

"There's more rat stew if you want it," Emily offered.

The goblins had begun packing their things, and Kate explained that the creatures—at least as far as she could tell from her pantomimed translation session—did not like being out under an open sky, so returning to the caves, and thus away from the human village, was as much in their own interest as it was to the villagers.

"How long have you been here," Jane asked Eric, who winced as he choked down more of the stew.

"I have no idea," he said. Seeing him outside the cavern light, he looked older than the group, and even more worse for wear than he'd appeared in the spider's web.

"So you've been trapped a long time?" Jane asked.

He shook his head, wrinkling his brow in thought.

"That's the funny thing," he said. "My friends and I... we didn't know we were trapped for a long time. This place—it was more fun than regular life, right? We had nothing to go back to, or at least nothing we wanted to go back to more than we wanted to stay here and be heroes. So we just went all in with it. Really played the roles. I mean... why go back to ordinary life when you can save villages from dragons and spend the night singing in an in with elves and halflings?"

"Your friends," Kate said, sitting down beside Titus. "How many of you were there?"

"Four," Eric said, setting his bowl aside. "We were the classic group makeup—a fighter, a cleric, a rogue, and a wizard. What are all of you?"

Titus pointed around the group.

"Paladin, monk, druid, ranger, and Emily," Titus said.

"Bard," Emily corrected.

"Wow. What, did you get the expansion pack or something?" Eric said.

"Expansion pack?" Billy said, his voice cracking.

"I think we're playing second edition," Emily said.

"You were saying, about your friends," Jane said, nudging the conversation back on track.

"Right," Eric said. "Well, none of us wanted to go home. I mean, dead end jobs, families who wouldn't really miss us… I mean, Kim worked retail. Why would she want to go home? Here she was the greatest fighter in the entire kingdom."

"So what happened?" Titus said.

"You know the old saying, it's all fun and games until…?" Eric said. "Well it was all fun and games until Nolan took an orc's arrow to his neck."

"What?" Billy said.

"He was casting a healing spell on Kim, not paying attention, and then…" Eric spread his hands out at his sides. "Then it stopped being a game."

"We can die here," Jane said.

"Very much so," Eric said. "Nolan was our cleric, so he kept us alive even when we got in over our heads. And we watched him bleed out in the muddy snow of Torvak Valley. We barely got out of there alive. But after that… we wanted to go home."

"But you couldn't," Kate said.

"Yes and no. We found out how," Eric said. "It really is a game, so all the rules are there if you look for them. Kill the big bad, end the game, go home."

He pointed east.

"And the game plays into all sorts of old-fashioned tropes. You've got to kill the dark wizard in the tower," Eric said.

"Did you try?" Jane asked.

"We did," Eric said. "But with just the three of us, with our confidence gone... we started making mistakes. John, our thief, was poisoned trying to pick a lock. Man, you guys look young, but if you're here you must remember how cheap it always felt when your thief got poisoned right? In the old days, thief characters were always getting themselves killed. Except poison is a terrible way to when you see it for real, right? It was awful."

"What happened to your other friend?" Jane asked.

"Here's the worst of it," Eric said. "All those victories we had? We made a lot of enemies. When they found out we were on the run, a lot of the villains we defeated came after us. That's how I ended up in that cave. Kim and I were running. She died fighting the undead. I ran deeper into the caves to hide."

"And then: spider chow," Billy said.

"Until you showed up," Eric said. "So look, I don't know what to tell you. Thanks, first of all, but also: I'm sorry. I don't know if we're ever meant to beat this game."

"Fortunately for you, Eric the Mage, we are actual, honest-to-goodness heroes in real life," Emily said. "This was supposed to be a team building exercise."

"We're going to get out of this game," Kate said.

"And we're going to take you with us," Jane said.

"However, if you have a map telling us where this evil wizard is, that'd be huge," Billy said.

Eric shook his head in disbelief, a pained smile on his face.

"That I can do," Eric said. "Man, I hope you're not delusional."

Chapter 11: Good citizens

They made their way back to the town the next day, returning to the tavern where they'd first heard of the goblins. A cheer went up as they entered.

"Oh no," Kate said, wilting and hovering by the door.

"This is like a social anxiety nightmare," Titus said.

"You two," Emily said, stomping in and throwing her arms up in the air.

"The goblin threat is no more!" she yelled. The patrons cheered again.

The mayor, dressed much the same as when they last saw her, made her way up to the front of the tavern and handed Emily a mug.

"Did you kill them all?" she asked.

"Kill?" Emily said.

"Um," Jane said. Emily fired Billy a warning look, and he took Jane by the arm and pulled her away from the mayor.

"Now is not the time for your inability to tell a lie to rear its ugly head," Billy whispered.

"Why do you two always find honest a negative quality?" she rasped back at him.

Titus, getting a good read of the room, put a hand on Emily's shoulder.

"Every last one of them," he said. "The goblins fought well for the little monsters they are, but they've been exterminated. Your village is safe."

"Did you give 'em what for?" a gruff-voiced man yelled from the far wall of the tavern.

"Oh, we gave 'em!" Emily said. "Why our druid used his magic to transform into a dire wolf and must've killed oh, fifteen of them single handedly."

"Fifteen? Billy yelled, pointing a threatening finger at Jane to stay quiet. "He only killed fifteen if you counted with one eye. He must've killed twice that."

"Well then, dinner's on the house, brave adventurers!" the stout bartender hollered. "Clarence, clear these heroes a table. Mabel, bring out roast and potatoes for them, and don't skimp on the butter."

A bent-backed man shooed a group of happy drunks away from a long table while a young serving girl scurried to the back for their food.

Sheepishly, the Indestructibles sat down around the newly empty table. Kate leaned in to Emily grimly.

"And what happens when the goblins we killed come back in a few days?" Kate said.

"Trust me, in games like this, goblins reproduce like ants. New tribes are always popping up. They'll just assume it's a new goblin infestation. It's why there's *always* a goblin problem," Emily said.

"I never want any of you to refer to me as the harsh one again," Kate said, sitting down next to Jane, with whom she exchanged commiserating looks.

Emily took a sip of the mug she'd been handed, grimaced, and set it aside.

"This is not butterbeer," she said. Billy took the cup from her and took a sip as well.

"Oh," he said, his mouth turning down. "Oh, that's not nice at all. I felt that in my soul. That's…"

"That's Bruno the bartender's house special, so don't make fun of it too loudly," the mayor said, joining them. "But to be fair, it's pretty unpleasant stuff. Keeps you warm on a cold night though."

She set a nondescript sack down on the table between them.

"Payment, as promised. We scrounged together everything we could as your reward. Everyone in town pitched in," she said.

"You keep that," Jane said.

"Jane!" Emily said, appalled.

"You need it more than we do, to rebuild," Jane said.

"She really is a paladin," Billy said. "She's been a paladin the entire time we've known her."

"Jane, you can't just…" Emily said. Jane hooked Emily by the collar of her shirt.

"A moment, bard?" Jane said.

Emily made a "just a second" gesture to the mayor.

"My paladin wants a consultative meeting," she said.

Pulling Emily just far enough to be inaudible to the mayor under the din of the bar's crowd, Jane whispered into Emily's ear.

"We're leaving," she said. "Why should we take these peoples' gold when we're going to back to reality tomorrow?"

Emily's mouth opened and closed a few times. "That… is a very good point."

"So, we don't take their money. We get to be big heroes. They don't go broke paying us for goblins which we did not kill, by the way…"

"Ixnay on the oblins-gay, Ane-jay," Emily said.

"Pig Latin isn't a particularly effective spy tool," Billy said, joining them. Dude, still in owl form and looking like a feathery ball of belligerence, perched on his shoulder. "I have an idea."

"No," Jane said.

"Trust me," Billy said.

He returned to the table and picked up the bag of gold, which he gently placed in the mayor's hands.

"What we did, we did to save your community. We need no financial rewards," Billy said. "If you could, though—we're about to embark on another adventure, and could use some provisions for the road. Perhaps a change of clothes for our new friend over there whom we rescued from the spi—"

"Goblins," Titus interrupted.

"From the goblins," Billy said. "But gold will only slow us down, and I'm sure the children of the village have a greater need of it than we do."

"What is he doing," Kate said, leaning in to Titus.

"Every once in a while Billy's not an idiot," Titus said.

The mayor set the money down on the table again, looked at each member of the party in turn, then gave Billy a warm, motherly hug.

"You really are sent by the gods, aren't you," she said.

"I get that a lot," Billy said.

Titus put his head on the table and groaned.

"We'll get you set up proper," the mayor said. "Dried goods for the road, proper water skins, and by the gods above, look at the shoes on your man over there—we'll get your new friend a proper pair of boots. Bless you all."

Billy looked around the group, grinning like a fool. Jane smiled at him proudly—which made him feel a sense of pride he was almost embarrassed by—and even Kate raised an approving eyebrow at him.

"Can I ask you all, though," the mayor said, putting a kindly hand on Titus's arm. "Where is your next adventure taking you? More goblin slaying? Maybe into the swamp to fight off the trolls there?"

"We're headed east to defeat an evil wizard," Jane said.

The woman removed her hand from Titus's shoulder, made a strange symbol in the air, and spat on the ground. Her face filled with worry.

"Bah, and I was just warming up to you," she said. "No one ever comes back from that tower. I wish you wouldn't. We can keep you busy here if you'd rather. The next town over has problems with kobolds in their mines…"

"It's a battle we have to take on," Jane said.

"That's what they all say," the mayor said, picking up Emily's still-full mug and downing the contents. "Well, you were a good lot. I'll wish you the best of luck. If anyone wants to leave letters to send home to your families to say goodbye, we'll be happy to get them where they need going."

Chapter 12: The eagleboar

They left town the next day, headed west away from the town. The mayor wished them good luck and gave them provisions, but made sure to say that she didn't need the bag those provisions were compiled in back, because "nobody comes back from the tower anyway." Jane thanked her profusely. Billy made a joke about optimism. Kate did not.

A few hours out, the forest around them began to change noticeably. The trees grew more twisted and gnarled; the leaves darker, often resembling strips of leather hanging from the branches. The path they followed became harder to traverse, with roots and rocks jutting up as if intending to trip them.

"I swear that tree is looking at me," Titus said, pointing. Kate walked up to the tree in question, studying it, then backed away slowly.

"Let's keep going," she said.

"What?" Jane asked.

"I think the tree winked at me," Kate said.

"You're kidding," Eric said.

Titus shook his head.

"Stick around long enough, you'll learn that she never kids," he said.

Billy lifted his hand in the air and Dude fluttered down out of the sky and landed on his wrist, awkwardly hopping onto Billy's shoulder.

"Did Dude see anything?" Jane asked.

Billy shrugged.

"Our psychic bond is blocked," Billy said. "And I'm able to pick up on some of what the hoots mean, but he's not exactly crystal clear about what one hoot means versus another."

"You call the owl 'dude?'" Eric said.

"Back in the real world, he's not an owl," Billy said. "He's an alien… you know what? That's too long a story to tell right now."

"We're trapped in a board game," Eric said. "You tell me the owl is an alien, I'm inclined to believe you. Get your metagame on for all I care."

Billy squinted, looking further up the trail.

"I'm going to scout ahead," Billy said.

"And I'm going to break into a musical number," Titus said. "When have you ever been a scout?"

"Look at me!" Billy said, gesturing at his costume. "I'm a ranger. I'm going to range."

"This is a game, Billy," Jane said.

"Yeah, but in the real world I've never shot a bow and arrow and here I'm a bullseye," Billy said. "Emily doesn't know how to play any musical instruments in the real world. How does she know how to play a lute? We have the appropriate abilities here for our roles. I'm going to scout ahead."

"He has a point," Emily said.

"You do not get to weigh in on major decisions. It's your fault we're here," Jane said.

"I'll come with you," Titus said.

"You are the least stealthy person I've ever known in my life," Kate said. "You walk like you have bricks tied to your shoes."

"In the real world," Titus said, stealing Billy's term. "Here I'm a druid. Master of the wilds. I can pass silently through the wilderness."

"We are going to have a really long talk when we get home," Kate said.

"Go on," Jane said. "Just... be careful. Don't do anything stupid."

"We won't," Billy said.

"Titus, don't let Billy do anything stupid," Jane corrected.

Titus nodded, and the boys headed further up the trail and were soon out of sight.

"So, I've been thinking," Emily said.

Kate sighed.

"No, no," Emily said. "Seriously. The mayor said no one ever comes back from the wizard's tower, right? What if that means that they all go home? Maybe their town is on the path to the end of the game?"

"Or everyone who goes to the tower dies," Kate said.

"Why are you so cheerful all the time?" Emily snarked.

"She could be right," Eric said. "But honestly... This game escalates. You get confident, you're having fun, and then suddenly... it turns on you. I think we're going to find a pile of dead bodies at that tower."

"We found another optimist, then," Emily said.

"But we're going into this knowing we're headed somewhere dangerous. We know the stakes," Jane said. "And I know we don't look like it, Eric, but we're fighters. In the real world. We've faced worse."

"Stormed a lot of wizards' castles, have you?" Eric said, smirking sheepishly.

"Near enough," Jane said.

Emily cracked open a bottle of water and wondered if they could catch anything by drinking it here. They walked perhaps another mile before they heard a crash in the distance.

"I think your boyfriend didn't keep Billy out of trouble," Emily said to Kate.

"Is that... coming this way?" Eric said. He readied a staff they were able to pick up in town before leaving, a poor replacement for the magician's staff he'd lost in the spider caves, but he had assured them he could still play his role in a fight if needed.

Another crash echoed through the air, and another. Jane drew her sword.

"Billy Case, what did you do," she said.

Then they found out exactly what Billy Case did.

He came flying out of the underbrush, leaves in his hair, eyes wild, his bow in hand. Dude flapped beside him in a manic flurry of white feathers.

"Where's Titus?" Kate said.

"Run! Run everybody run right now run!" Billy said.

"Where's..." Kate said again, but then she got her answer.

Following on Billy's heels was a monster none of them had ever seen before. It was the size of a small car with the body of a wild boar, thickly muscled and covered in course black hair. Its head, however, was not a boar's but rather that of an eagle, whose oversized beak was determined to snap Billy in half.

Titus was on the creature's back, in full werewolf form, jaws biting into its flesh less to hurt the monster and more as an attempt to not go flying off into the forest as the monster bucked and thrashed.

"I got this!" Emily yelled, throwing her arms out in front of her.

Nothing happened.

"No bubble of float! I have no powers here! I forgot!" Emily said. "I made a mistake!"

Kate stepped forward calmly. Billy ran past her, dropping to his knees and pulling an arrow from his quiver, spinning to let fly. He missed entirely, his glowing arrow skipping and spinning off into the distance. Jane started to charge, her shield up, bracing for impact.

Kate reached back, and calmly threw a single, silent punch at the creature's forehead, her body a fountain of stillness.

There was a sickening, brutal thump as her fist connected with the monster's face. Physics dictated that she should have been trampled; but instead, the monster stopped dead in its tracks as if it had slammed into a stone wall. Its body continued forward, lifting upward, flipping in the air, sending Titus spinning off into the distance. The creature made an almost graceful arc in the air, flying over Kate's unmoving form and coming to a crashing halt behind her.

Its legs twitched, kicking into the air. But the monster itself did not get back up. Dust, rocks, and assorted debris kicked up by the impact fell quietly all around Kate. Emily, also knocked off her feet by the crash, sat up.

"How did you do that," she said.

"Billy," Kate said.

"What?" Billy said.

"You said we all know how to do things here we don't back home. I'm playing the role of some sort of mystical martial artist. Somehow I knew…"

"That you were One Punch Man?" Emily said.

At the edge of the path, Titus, now transformed back into his human shape, stood up shakily and brushed leaves and dirt off his clothes.

"What was that thing?" Jane asked.

"It's an eagleboar," Eric said. "Classic creature from the game we're trapped in. Players hate them because they're usually a tough fight."

"I can vouch for that," Titus said. Kate glared at him. "You having fun yet?"

"No," Kate said.

"What did you do to make it mad, anyway?" Jane said.

"Nothing! We just looked at it!" Billy said.

"Yeah, that's part of the game mechanic," Eric explained. "Eagleboars are belligerent by nature."

"So glad we know that now," Titus said. He spat on the ground, and bits of dirt and dust came with it.

"On the upside," Billy said. "I think we found the path to the tower."

Chapter 13: The stone forest

The creepiness of the forest became almost quaint once they found the next leg of their journey. Passing through a narrow, claustrophobia-inducing path between two rocky outcroppings, they left the haunted forest behind them and arrived in a place that had the makings of a hellscape.

The ground on the other side of the chasm was black as soot, made up of stone and gravel. Instead of trees, stalagmites jutted up from the ground like teeth. The ground let off faint steam in places, as if magma were just below the surface.

"I don't think I could've thought this up in a nightmare," Titus said.

"We are literally going to Mordor, aren't we," Emily said.

"I've changed my mind," Billy said. "We don't have to go home. We can go back to the village and spend the rest of our days rescuing villagers from goblins and just accept that this is our reality now. I'm good."

Kate pushed past all of them and went forward wordlessly. Everyone turned to Jane for direction. She shrugged and followed Kate's lead.

"We can't stay her, in any event," Jane said. Everyone else fell in line behind her.

"Maybe I should scout ahead," Billy said.

Eric laughed. Billy shot him a wounded expression.

"It went so well last time," Emily said. "What happened, anyway?"

"Billy peed on the eagleboar," Titus said.

Jane stopped dead in her tracks. Emily crashed into her back. Billy tripped over Emily.

"What?" Jane said.

"We stopped for a break and..." Titus said.

"He looked like a rock, okay?" Billy said. "I thought I was peeing on a rock that looked sort of like a pig, not a giant boar with an eagle for a head."

Dude hooted indignantly on Billy's shoulder. Billy glared at him.

"I don't even speak owl and I know you just said something judgmental," Billy said to the owl.

"Guys," Jane said, pointing ahead where Kate had stopped to examine something on the ground. The group picked up its pace to meet her.

"I think the theory about a lot of people dying trying to get home is right," Kate said as they arrived.

Splayed on the ground were six skeletons in various states of battle damage. Most wore armor of some kind; one had colorful robes, now faded, and a pointed hat.

Eric leaned over and took a staff from the last skeleton's hand. It was ornate, wrote in gold, with a reddish wood as its base component.

"This is a high-level magic item," Eric said. "These guys weren't messing around."

Emily kicked at a shield one of the skeletons still held in its hand. The shield fell over with a clank.

"What killed 'em?" she asked.

"Well, it wasn't starvation," Jane said. She pointed at punctures in the plate armor on one of the dead adventurers and looked to Eric. "Any idea what we're fighting out here?"

"Nothing I've seen in this game is illogical," Eric said. "And my friends and I traveled all over. Whatever is out here would make sense in this environment. My first guess would be maybe fire or stone elementals, but these look like sword or spear wounds."

"Teeth," Titus said.

"What?" Kate said.

"No," Billy said. "Absolutely not. That tooth would have to be the size of my hand to make a hole that big."

"It's a bite mark," Titus said. Kate squinted at him, doubtful. "Look, if I know one thing, it's bite wounds, right? It's my line of work. These guys lost a fight with something…"

Kate knelt down to examine the bodies further. She lifted a piece of platemail with a curved series of puncture wounds.

"Something with a mouth big enough to do that," she said.

"Giant monsters," Billy said. "No problem. We've fought giant monsters before. Lots of giant monsters."

"In game?" Eric said.

"In real life," Emily said.

"Though we had our powers all those other times," Jane said.

"Nothing to worry about," Billy said. "We've got our gear."

"We're all going to die," Emily said.

"Yep," Titus said. "And it's all your fault."

Chapter 14: It's not a dragon, exactly

The conversation took a noticeable dip after finding the corpses, with even Emily not saying much. At one point, she started fiddling with her lute, but Kate put a threatening hand on the instrument, and Emily put it away.

They saw few signs of life. Oversized centipedes scurried around in the blackened dust. Occasionally a bird would drift overhead, looking to scavenge. The journey ran the risk of almost becoming boring.

Then Titus stopped.

"You've got to be kidding me," he said, pointing at the sky in front of them.

"What," Billy said. "What could you possibly have spotted that has finally kicked off your sense of disbelief?"

"I'm guessing that," Jane said, following Titus's gaze. Billy did the same.

"Oh, come on," he said. "Is that a dragon?"

The creature drifted through the air on massive, leathery wings, a head full of fangs looking around at the end of a long neck. Its two back legs were tucked up tight against its abdomen, while a long tail, sharply pointed at the end, seemed to help the creature swim through the sky.

"It's not a dragon, exactly," Emily said. "I'm pretty sure it's a wyvern."

"It looks like a dragon to me," Billy said.

"No, see how it's got two back legs and its front legs are basically the wings, like a bird? That's a wyvern. A dragon has front and back legs plus wings too," Titus said.

Kate stared at him like she barely recognized him.

"We really do have so much to talk about when we get home about the things you get up to when I'm not around," she said.

"What's a wyvern, then," Jane said. "Like a fancy dragon?"

"Honestly, there're like dumb dragons," Eric said. "In this world, dragons are smarter than humans. They can talk, and scheme, and interfere. Wyverns are… well, if dragons are smarter than people, wyverns are smart as dogs."

"That's a relief, sort of," Jane said.

"I dunno. Dogs are pretty smart," Emily said. "At least as smart as Billy. Possibly smarter."

"Really? We're doing insult comedy right now?" Billy said.

"There's got to be a way to sneak around it," Titus said.

"Right! This is clearly a high level encounter we're supposed to avoid. We'll just roll for stealth," Emily said.

"We'll roll for what?" Jane said.

"We'll do a stealth check and see if we pass," Emily said.

"We're not actually playing a game, Emily," Titus said. "There's no dice here. "

"I'd like to think somewhere back home our real bodies are rolling dice," Emily said.

"Have you been thinking about this the whole time?" Jane said.

"Maybe," Emily said.

Billy interrupted the conversation by putting a hand on Jane's shoulder.

"Uh-oh," Billy said pointing at the wyvern.

"I don't even want to look," Kate muttered.

"Our stealth check failed, huh," Emily said.

The monster definitely, without a doubt, had spotted them. It circled around in the sky like a pinwheel and turned its attention in their direction, flying right at them.

"I guess he's back for his noon feeding," Emily said.

Kate turned her head left to right.

"These stalagmites will offer some cover," she said.

"From a giant flying lizard," Billy said, pulling an arrow from his quiver. "What am I doing. This is why the archers always die in comics, isn't it? Draw aggro from the bad guys at range before the tank can get in there?"

"Wait!" Emily yelled. She slipped her lute from her back and strummed the strings. "I know what to do."

"We're gonna need a bigger lute!" Billy said.

"Hey, that's my line," Emily said. "And I have a charm spell!"

"A what? A—you and charm in the same sentence doesn't fill me with confidence," Billy said.

"I'm listening, Em," Jane said, drawing her sword and setting her shield at the ready. "What do you need."

"I just need to… it's a magic song. I can charm him. It's like hypnotizing him. He'll be on our side!" Emily said.

Jane stepped in front of Emily and lifted her shield.

"Then start playing, Emily," Jane said.

Once again, the fact that Emily could play the instrument in this world was more than a little off-putting for all of her teammates, but play she could, a lilting, lovely tune. Even Kate looked mildly impressed.

The wyvern's flight began to slow a little. Its eyes looked less ferocious; in as much as any of them could read its body language, it even seemed a little less aggressive.

"This just might work," Eric said.

Then Emily started singing.

If her lute-playing skills in this world were impossibly high, her singing voice was just the opposite. Squeaking, off-rhythm, and more than a little tone-deaf, the sound of her voice sent chills up the spines of her friends.

"Oh, wow," Titus said.

"You're even worse here than in the real world," Billy said.

The wyvern appeared to be shaken from the hypnotic sound of the lute and began flying toward them faster.

"I think I forgot to put points into the singing skill!" Emily said.

"What do we do, guys," Jane said.

"Someone else sing!" Emily said. "I think it'll work if someone else sings!"

"What if nobody else can sing here!" Titus said. He turned to Billy. "I can't sing, can you sing?"

"I don't know! Can you?" Billy asked Eric.

"I listen to death metal! I don't think this calls for death metal singing!" Eric said, looking fearful for the first time.

"Jane," Kate said.

"I'm ready," Jane said.

"No. You can sing," Kate said. "We've all heard you."

"Are you serious?" Jane said. "What do I sing? Emily, I don't know the words to the magic spell!"

The wyvern was so close its enormous wings kicked up dust and debris into their faces. It radiated a strange, alien heat.

"Sing anything!" Emily said.

Jane, out of nowhere, broke into a pitch-perfect rendition of the "Rainbow Connection."

The wyvern stopped dead in its tracks, flapping its massive wings to stay airborne just meters from them.

"It's working!" Emily said.

"As long as I live I will never have an experience this strange ever again," Eric said.

"I hope for all our sakes you're right about that," Kate said.

The wyvern found a clearing among the stalagmites and landed. It snaked its long head toward Jane, who tensed, but kept singing. When the monster butted its head against her like a cat, she almost lost the song, but maintained.

"How long does she have to keep singing, Em?" Titus said.

"I... think you can stop now," Emily said.

"What's the spell duration?" Eric asked.

"I think it's twenty-four hours, unless we hurt it," Emily said.

"Okay, then. For twenty-four hours, we have a dog-dragon," Billy said.

"Pretty much," Emily said.

They all stood around looking slightly lost.

"Can we ride it?" Kate asked.

Chapter 15: They always go through the sewers

The wyvern took them across the blackened landscape quickly, as dark spires of stone and rivulets of magma passed silently below. It did not take long for a tower—tall and gray, dotted with high, narrow windows, seemingly grown out of the ground like the stalk of an angry plant—appeared on the horizon. Emily commanded the hypnotized wyvern to land what she hoped as a safe distance from the tower.

As soon as they landed, Titus slid off and walked to the nearest stalagmite, using it for support.

"You're not going to be sick, are you?" Emily said.

Titus waved her off.

"He's still afraid of flying," Kate said.

"Three teammates who literally fly and a base that is a spaceship floating miles above our city and he's still got a thing about heights," Billy said. "Amazing."

"I'm not sick, and I'm not afraid," Titus said. "And I can definitely hear everything all of you are saying."

Jane looked up at the still docile wyvern.

"What do we do with this guy," she said.

"We could have it fight for us," Eric suggested. "You're controlling a powerful monster. Could help defeat the dark wizard."

Jane grimaced.

"Not his fight," she said.

"Plus if he gets hurt there's a chance the enchantment will break and then we'll have a dark wizard and an angry wyvern on our hands," Emily said.

Jane put a hand on the creature's neck, admiring its scales. Up close, they were pearlescent gold-green.

"No reason for him to die for us," Jane said.

"He's not real," Eric said. "None this is real. It's all illusionary."

"Feels real," Jane said. "People die here for real too. Your friends were real."

"I've been here so long I sometimes wonder if I'm real," Eric said.

Kate cut the conversation off abruptly.

"What's our next move?" she said. "I see a door. We can have Titus kick it in."

"I think stealth is our better option," Emily said.

"You keep suggesting that, and it never works out," Billy chimed in.

"Six of us. Unknown threat level inside. She has a point," Kate said. "We could sneak in."

"There's always a sewer leading out of a place like this," Emily said. "In the stories, they always go through the sewers."

"Have I mentioned lately my superhuman sense of smell," Titus said.

"Better than kicking the door in," Jane said. "Titus, I assume you can..."

"Yes, heavens help me, I can find the sewer exit with my nose," Titus said. "I hate my life sometimes."

Once again, Jane looked up to admire the winged creature beside her.

"I wish we could keep him," she said.

"If I were dungeon master of this game, I would definitely let you find a way to keep your wyvern," Emily said.

"But you're not," Jane said.

"Nope."

"What do we do, then?"

Emily petted the wyvern's neck. The creature turned its attention on the diminutive hero.

"Go find yourself a good lunch, big guy," Emily said. "We're going to be a while, so take your time. Have the best day of your life. Okay? Ride the warm air, eat a water buffalo, roll around in a big open field of flowers. The good stuff."

The wyvern seemed to comprehend the intent of the command, if not the words. With a gust of wind, he took off, soon disappearing on the horizon.

"The spell will wear off in a few hours," Emily said. "I figured I should put him in a good mood. Also send him far enough away he won't come looking for us."

"So games like this can be fun sometimes, huh?" Jane said.

"It's all about how you play," Emily said.

Chapter 16: The worst thing we've ever done

"Guys," Emily said as they sloshed through the slowly moving waters beneath the tower. Titus had found an outflow pipe and now, their path lit by Jane's sword and a pair of light spells cast by Eric and Titus, the group trudged onward miserably.

"Guys," Emily repeated. "In all my years of role playing games, I've been in a lot of sewers. In game, I mean."

"That's nice, Em," Jane said, her voice catching in her throat at the smell surrounding them.

"Like, a lot of sewers. And let me tell you, no matter how talented a game master I was playing with, no matter how in-depth the descriptive powers of the players, I have never fully appreciated how bad sewers can smell."

"Yup," Titus said, the nausea in his voice almost overtaking him.

"Guys, we're in a sewer. This is horrible."

"Yes, it is, Emily," Billy said.

"Do you even know what we're stepping in right now?" Emily said. "I mean seriously, this right here, this is—"

"Stop," Kate said.

Emily paused. She didn't stop.

"This is the worst thing we've ever been through," Emily said. And we've seen some stuff."

"Everyone be quite for a minute," Titus said suddenly.

"By everyone, you mean Emily," Billy said.

Titus hushed him.

"Do you hear that?" Titus said a moment later.

"That... sounded like moaning," Eric said.

"Would a dark wizard use... zombies to guard his tower?" Titus said.

"I wouldn't put it past him," Eric said. "Could be any number of different types of undead though. The options are pretty endless."

"I love zombie movies," Emily said.

"Living dead? I'm gonna be honest. Not a fan," Billy said.

"Keep talking. Maybe they'll hear us and you'll see them face to face," Kate said.

Billy and Emily both fell silent. The group plodded onward, eventually finding a stone staircase leading up.

"Are we... we're going up, aren't we," Titus said.

"Could just hang out in the sewer for a while," Billy said.

Jane brushed past them and climbed the stairs, pushing open a wooden trap door above. She lifted it just far enough to get a look at the room above.

"I don't see—" Jane started to say. Then the door was yanked open from above and a massive, graying hand grabbed Jane by the upper body and lifted her entirely out of sight.

"Jane!" Emily yelled.

Kate was first through the hatch, followed immediately by Titus, who had already begun transforming. The others caught up to see a scene that might have been funny in other circumstances: a massive creature, clearly made of the stitched-together parts of many oversized humanoid creatures, held Jane in the air like a wayward cat. Jane kicked and swung her sword, but the monster's arm was long enough to make sure her flaming sword couldn't reach.

"Flesh golem," Eric said.

"Frankenstein?" Billy said.

"Pretty much actually," Emily said. "Flesh golems are pretty mindless. I don't think I have a song that'll lull him into our pet, guys."

Kate raced forward, bashing the monster in the back of the knee with her staff. The creature staggered a bit, but otherwise shrugged off the blow as if it were a gentle push. Titus launched into the air, claws and fangs ready to tear into the monster, but the golem swung a mighty arm and sent the werewolf flying through the air and into a nearby stone wall.

Billy let fly one of his glowing arrows, which hit the creature dead in the chest, burning the frayed skin and muscle there. The monster moaned in pain.

"At least he's not a zombie!" Billy said, nocking another arrow.

"Get your friend out of there," Eric said. "I think I know how to stop it."

Billy fired again, this time sending the arrow through the wrist of the hand holding Jane aloft. Again, the monster let out a groaning sound of pain, but his grip held firm.

Then Titus reappeared, clamping down on the creature's arm and tearing at it with his claws. The golem let Jane drop to the ground as it grabbed Titus with its other hand and slammed him to the ground brutally. Titus let out a sound not unlike one might hear from a kicked dog.

Eric muttered a quick incantation and aimed his open palm at the creature. A ball of flame erupted from his hand, smashing into the golem's upper torso. The undead thing flailed around, blinded, as the stitching holding it together began to fray and give way. Eric launched another fireball, finishing the golem off.

"Smells like burning dog hair in here," Emily said.

"That would be me," Titus said, laying on the ground in human form. He looked a little singed and definitely bloodied, but otherwise not in bad condition. "That fireball got a little too close for comfort."

"Sorry about that," Eric said sheepishly.

"You wouldn't be the first person to accidentally beat me up while I was in my werewolf form," Titus said as Kate helped him back to his feet.

"So that... that's..." Eric said, making a vague gesture at Titus's frame.

"Yeah, that carried over from the real world," Titus said. "Congratulations! Werewolves are real. We get a lot of bad publicity."

The group pulled themselves back together, Emily helping Jane adjust her now-dented armor, Billy handing Titus the spear he'd abandoned when he transformed.

"Okay," Jane said, coughing. "Let's not do that again. What's next?"

She looked up. Everyone else followed her gaze. Billy swore. Above them, instead of normal stairs, the tower was lined with something out of an M.C. Escher sketch, with stairways sideways, upside down, bending back into themselves, chaos of geometry.

"This goes against everything about how my brain works," Kate muttered.

"I got this. I can get this," Emily said. "I spend half my life floating upside down or sideways. I think in four dimensions."

"That doesn't... there isn't... never mind," Titus said.

"Do we really have to go up there?" Billy said. "I..."

Before he could finish his thought, Dude, whom everyone had all but forgotten during the battle, fluttered down in a flapping mess of owl feathers and landed on Billy's shoulders, startling him.

"Gah! Dude! Come on! I wasn't ready!" Billy said.

"I think he's trying to tell you something," Jane said.

The owl hooted once, looked up, hooted again, then looked up once more.

"That's it. That's the message. We have to go up," Billy said. "You are an enormous help, Dude. Thanks for that."

Emily trotted over to the nearest staircase, which began on the ground level properly, but quickly changed angles to appear as if one needed to walk on the wall to continue. Emily put her foot on the unnaturally-angled steps and continued walking.

And suddenly she stood on the wall, perpendicular to the floor.

"See? We just need to take the magic stairs!" Emily said, grinning wildly.

Jane sighed deeply.

"I miss being able to fly," she said.

Chapter 17: The big bad

It took hours to climb the M.C. Escher stairs, almost entirely uneventful, except for one uncomfortable moment when Emily somehow took a wrong turn and ended up on the opposite side of the tower, looking up, and over, at her teammates. They backtracked, another stomach-churning process which Titus described as reversing direction on a playground roundabout after having already spun so fast to have induced nausea, found Emily, and continued on their way.

Everyone at some point took a moment to look down to the bottom of the tower, which was, for the most part, open on the interior, so no matter where you were on the stairs, you could see the ground growing further and further away.

"We couldn't play Monopoly, could we, Em?" Titus said.

"I don't even want to imagine how a game of 'Monopoly' in Doc's office could be cursed," Jane said.

"What about 'Life?'" Billy said. "Would a cursed game of 'Life' just trap us in really ordinary lives where instead of having super powers we just... grow up and have regular lives?"

By the time they reached the end of the twisted staircase, they were finally properly vertical on a stone landing. Titus leaned against the wall. Billy looked over the edge.

"We are so far up," Billy said.

"This tower is definitely bigger on the inside," Emily said.

Before them, another, shorter staircase led up to a wooden hatch in the ceiling. Jane shook her head.

"I'm not going through first," she said.

"You're the tank. You're supposed to go first," Emily said.

"Last time I went first, a Frankenstein on performance enhancing drugs lifted me up by my head," Jane said.

"Right. That's your job. You're the tank. You're our meat shield," Emily said.

"I'm your what?" Jane said, appalled.

Kate made her way past them and pushed the hatch open with her staff.

"I'll go first," Kate said.

Emily gestured at Kate she disappeared into the hatch.

"Sometimes monks go first," Emily said.

Titus and Eric followed, then Jane—wrinkling her nose at Emily and muttering meat shield—with Emily and Billy bringing up the rear.

They stepped into a fully decked out magician's laboratory. Strange potions bubbled over burners; tomes lined shelves that looked barely capable of holding them. Candlelight, glittering from tall, plain candles bathed the entire room in a soft, golden light. A dragon's head was mounted on the wall like one might find a moose on the wall in a winter cabin.

"Nice set up. Clearly, he subscribes to 'Better Tomes and Gardens,'" Emily said.

"You people voluntarily hang out with her?" Eric said.

"Define voluntarily," Titus said.

A new voice joined the conversation, Shakespearean with a hard to place accent.

"I have to say, I'm almost impressed. It's been a long time since a band of adventurers made it all the way to my lab," the newcomer said.

He was an older man, with a long, graying beard and a ridiculous metal skullcap. He wore red robes adorned with mysterious symbols and carried a gnarled staff that felt more like a prop than a tool to support him as he walked.

"You made it past my maze, and my wyvern… tell me you didn't destroy my golem," he said.

"We did," Jane said. "And we're here to defeat you."

"Pity," the dark wizard said. "But to be honest, the golem was stitched together from the bodies of the last adventurers who came to my gates."

He sniffed dismissively.

"Or came through the sewers. You all smell ghastly."

"Sorry to offend your delicate sensibilities," Billy said.

"I have to ask," the wizard said. "Why do adventurers seek me out? This world may be a prison, but it's a beautiful one. You could live forever here as storybook heroes."

"People need us back home," Jane said.

"I've met so many adventurers like you," the wizard said. "And you want to know the hard truth of it? None of them, not one, was truly needed back home. The world moves on without us, little adventurers. We're missed briefly, we're mourned... and then, in the end, we're forgotten. Why die trying to get back to a world that won't miss you?"

"Oh, enough of this," Eric snapped. He aimed his magician's staff at the wizard and fired a blast of lightning at him, engulfing the villain in bluish light. The dark wizard laughed.

"I know you," he said, pointing at Eric like the younger man had just told a bad joke. "I've been waiting for you."

"I've been here long enough. I'm going to kill you, and I'm going home," Eric said.

"You know I can't let you do that," the dark wizard said.

And then, as if from nowhere, Kate stood behind the wizard, launching the mystic punch she'd used on the eagleboar at the back of his head.

The wizard caught a look in someone's eye—Jane's jaw had dropped the split second she saw Kate move into position—and swung around just in time to dodge most of the blow. The metal of his skullcap rang out like a bell.

"It always comes to this," the wizard said. He waved a hand at Kate and sent her sprawling against a nearby wall.

The rest of the Indestructibles leapt into action. Jane charged, flaming sword in hand. The wizard sent an icy blast to stop her, which she deflected with her shield, though the attack pushed her away. Titus cast a druid spell to tangle the wizard's feet in mystical vines, which withered as they touched the villain's boots. Giving up on the magical approach, Titus swiftly transformed into his werewolf form and charged, but the wizard called down a bolt of lightning of his own from the sky. Titus instinctually skittered out of the way of the blast, but the impact of lightning on stone caused the werewolf to be knocked off his feet.

Two blazing arrows streaked through the air and landed firmly in the wizard's torso, one in his shoulder, the other in his chest. The wizard grunted and simply yanked them out. As the wounds bled, the wizard touched his own blood and pointed at Billy, who dropped to his knees, groaning in agony.

"Pain for pain," the wizard said. "Not my favorite spell, but effective."

Before the wizard could continue gloating, a glass vial filled with bright blue fluid smashed against his head. He whipped around in a rage.

"What was that!" he growled. Then another vial, this one containing yellow fluid, exploded on his chest.

"I have no idea what any of these do, but I'm guessing none of them are good," Emily said.

The wizard opened his mouth to yell at her, but he was cut off as a bright orange vial crashed against his robes.

"No!" he said. "Stop! They—"

His robes burst into flames.

"Damn you!" the dark wizard yelled, blurting out a spell that dumped a cloud of rainwater down onto him, soaking his robes and putting out the chemical fire on his clothing. Much of the arcane lettering along one shoulder had been burned away. He saw Emily heft another vial and stopped her with a vicious twist of his hand, knocking the blue-haired bard over a table and out of sight.

More lightning crackled, but the dark wizard held up is staff, gathering the blue light and channeling it into the floor.

"You never do quit, do you," he said.

"You've kept me here too long," Eric said.

Jane yanked her shield free of the ice in time to see the dark wizard and the player mage face off. Eric had begun to change during the battle. His tattered robes looked more complicated, his beard darker and fuller; the simple staff he'd carried shifted into something more intricate and dangerous-looking. His eyes looked bruised, his cheeks hollow.

"This is a prison of your own making," the dark wizard said. "You know I can't let you leave."

"I know," Eric said. He banged his staff on the ground and a spike of ice shot from the floor, piercing the dark wizard's guts and pinning him in place. The wizard gasped and clutched at the wound, shocked.

"Well, this just got complicated," Billy said through gritted teeth. His breathing, previously shallow as his body was wracked by the pain spell, seemed to be returning to normal.

"Heel turn!" Emily said. She dragged herself back to her feet, leaning heavily on one of the tables on the far side of the room.

"You've been banished here for a reason, Edric," the dark wizard said.

"Edric?" Emily said. "Have we been saying his name wrong the whole time?"

"Edric of the Dark Pact. Warlock. Manipulator. Sentenced to stay in a cursed game he helped build. You are not allowed to go home," the dark wizard said.

"I hate being lied to," Jane said. She ran at Eric—Edric?—with her sword ready. He sent a shard of ice just like the one he used to impale the dark wizard at her, but she shunted the construct away with her shield, leaving the metal dented and warped. Billy fired an arrow that Edric sidestepped easily, before the warlock used a quick movement of his hand to topple a bookshelf onto Billy's back.

Titus and Kate closed in, the former letting out a low rumbling growl.

"Night creature. You're on the wrong side," Edric said. Kate said nothing, swinging her bo staff not to hit Edric but to slam down on his fingers, forcing him to release his own staff. The warlock cried out in annoyed pain, launching a lightning bolt at Kate in retaliation. Titus, without thinking, leapt in front of it, saving Kate but howling in pain as the electricity coursed through his monstrous body.

"You must stop him," the dark wizard said, growing pale, his voice little more than a croak.

"Five minutes ago, you weren't going to let us out of here," Jane said, circling Edric, her sword trailing flames behind it.

"That is just part of the game," the dark wizard said. "I am only following the script I was born to play out."

"Right, well, we'll figure out if people get to be evil because of a game in second. But first," Jane said. She dropped her shield and swung her sword with both hands, but Edric released a wave of mystical energy in all directions, sending her—and much of the room's contents—flying away from him.

"I'm so tired," Edric said. "I'm tired, and I'm bored, and I'm lonely, and I'm going home. Prepare to die, old man."

And then the room became bathed in purple light. A portal opened along one wall, and a welcome voice came through it.

"Are you people kidding me," Doc Silence said, stepping through the portal. His usual attire of long coat and jeans had been replaced, with a distinct lack of dignity, with deep blue wizard robes, though his signature red-lensed glasses remained in place. He wore a classic pointed wizard's hat. He reached up as if to check if the hat were really there, pulled it off his head, looked at it in disgust, and tossed it aside.

"Doc!" Emily said. "Hey, good to see you!"

"How many times have I told you everything in my office is dangerous?" Doc said.

"Never," Emily said. "Once. Okay maybe like fifty times."

"Silence," Edric said, turning a burning gaze on the newcomer.

"Stuff it, Edric," Doc said. "I'm not having this conversation again."

"You can't keep me trapped forever!"

"You know what? You're right," Doc said. "You've outsmarted this game. Time for another."

"What?" Edric said.

Another portal opened behind him. Jane could see just beyond the opening a desert sky, red sands.

"No," Edric said.

"If I could trust you to stop trying to destroy the world, I'd let you loose, man," Doc said. "But every time you get free you again, repeatedly, try to destroy the world. You're in a time out."

Edric raised his hands to attack, but Doc cast a spell as fast as a gunslinger, shoving the warlock's hands to his side.

"Jane, if you would," Doc said.

"Gladly," she said, and then she unceremoniously kicked the warlock through the open portal. Emily ran up beside her to watch just as the portal slammed shut.

"Whoa," Emily said. "Did you just banish him to a Dark Sun campaign? You are nasty, Doc. That's harsh."

"Harsh is the spell I'm going to cast on my office to turn you into a frog the next time you take something from it," Doc said. He walked up to the dying dark wizard and put a hand on his shoulder.

"You," the dark wizard said.

"Yup," Doc said. "You're dying."

"I am," the dark wizard said. "But I'll be back."

"You always are," Doc said.

"The dying is the worst part of this job," the dark wizard said. "No. No, the self-awareness is the worst part. Why did that happen?"

"A glitch in the magic," Doc said. "I'm sorry for that."

"Well then," the dark wizard said. "Until next time, you awful man."

The wizard slumped forward, expiring. Jane and Emily watched in curious horror as his body seemingly faded into nothing. A moment later, it was as if the dark wizard never existed.

"Doc," Billy said, crawling out from under the bookshelf. Dude flitted down to land on his head. "No need to deus ex machina this thing. We had it."

"No we did not," a pained Titus said, laying on the floor in his human form, nursing a nasty burn mark on his ribs where the lightning had hit. Kate helped him up. "You know, you never thank me when I take a lightning bolt for you."

"Thank you for taking a lightning bolt for me," Kate said.

"That sounded fake."

Kate shrugged.

Jane looked around at her team.

"So did we win the game?" she said.

"With a little dungeon master fudging of the die rolls," Emily said. "But really… does an RPG campaign ever really end?"

Chapter 18: Doing it right

"I'm not kidding," Doc said, as they returned to their own reality, appearing around the table exactly where they disappeared. Doc hunched over the table, putting pieces of the game away. "I will turn you into a toad if you steal things from my office, Emily. It's for your own safety."

"I know!" Billy said, not answering Doc's question but rather having a conversation entirely in his own head. "You know you missed me. What? No, I didn't miss you. Well, maybe a little bit."

He turned to the group and pointed at his forehead.

"Dude's back," he said. Then, once again answering Dude's voice in his mind: "What was it like being an owl? What? You know, you could trade me in for an owl if you liked it that much. It's not like owls are extinct or anything. Yeah, I thought so."

Jane shook her head and watched Billy pace and talk with Dude out of the corner of her eye.

"Doc," Jane said. "Why a board game? Why was Eric... um, Edric trapped in there?"

"Edric the Warlock," Doc said. "He's a villain I faced off with a long time ago. After the team and I stopped him a few times from taking over the real world, he got it in his head that if he couldn't control our world, he'd make one of his own to rule over. But he botched the spell. Magic has a way of punishing you for making mistakes."

"He made it sound like it's your fault he's trapped there," Titus said.

"Magic is also like math," Doc said. "Or code. I might have tweaked the equations of the magic he used to build a fantasy world to live in so that it wasn't the type of world he could either rule over, or leave."

"But you sent him somewhere else," Kate said.

"Unfortunately, the five of you are too good at your jobs," Doc said. "That final confrontation with the dark wizard weakened the binds that held him there. But I had a feeling that would happen eventually. So I found a place he could play his game without hurting anyone."

"To Dark Sun," Emily said. "That's Dungeons and Dragons for masochists and sociopaths."

"It's not literally a game world I sent him to," Doc said. "But it's not a gentle place, and it's one where magic is a bit of a competition. I think he'll actually fit in well there, because he'll have foes just like him, keeping each other busy."

"You sent him to evil wizard daycare?" Billy said, suddenly reconnecting with the conversation.

Doc raised an eyebrow and smirked.

"That's... that's pretty good, Billy," he said.

"I told you it was a good joke, Dude," Billy said to his alien companion.

Jane brushed her hand across the now empty table, watching as Doc sealed up the game box once more.

"I have to admit, though," Jane said. "It was pretty fun being a knight."

"I knew you'd like this sort of game!" Emily said.

"What happens to the world we just escaped?" Kate said. "Without Edric there, does it cease to exist?"

"It continues to be a real place," Doc said. "It's a pocket dimension. And Edric, for reasons I'll never know, created multiple copies. There's dozens of copies of the game out there in the real world. People playing it. I've never been able to find them all. And to be honest, now that he's not there, I'm not sure what to do."

"You can't destroy it," Jane said. "They might be game characters, but if you destroy it, that village disappears. Those goblins cease to exist. That's not fair."

Doc smiled at Jane with warmth and pride.

"You're right," he said. "Maybe with a little help from the right people, I can rewrite the equations to make it not so lethal for visitors from our world. I'll think about it.'

"I can't believe I'm saying this, but I think I'd like to go back," Jane said.

"I can't believe I'm agreeing with her, but me too," Titus said.

"Well, it's not safe to go back yet," Doc said, shaking the box. "It's not designed for recreational use... understood, Emily?"

"Why is this my fault?" Emily said.

"Because it's literally your fault," Titus said.

Doc glanced around at each of them, shaking his head.

"Okay," he said, and walked out of the room.

"Are we in trouble?" Billy asked, rejoining the table.

"Emily's in trouble," Titus said.

"Nobody's in trouble," Jane said. "Cut it out."

Doc returned with a couple of large hardcover books, a stack of paper, and a handful of pens.

"What's this now," Kate asked.

"You want to play a game?" Doc said. "Then we're doing it right."

"You're going to play a tabletop game with us?" Emily said.

"What else are we going to do with our evening?" Doc said. "You've already defeated a super villain."

Jane laughed.

"You promise this one won't take our powers away and trap us in a pocket dimension?" Jane said.

"Only in your imagination," Doc said. "Are you in?"

"No," Kate said.

"Yes, you are," Jane said.

"Fine," Kate said. "But I want to do that punching thing again."

"That can be arranged," Emily said. "Can I be a multiclass elf rogue/fighter/mage with a focus on Transmutation?"

Doc sighed, but there was no irritation in it.

"I'll see what I can do," he said. "So. Shall we begin?"

Preview:
The Players Guide to Dungeon Crawling

The Indestructibles are not the only people to find themselves trapped in the cursed board game appearing in *Roll for Initiative*.

What happens when six friends—ordinary role-playing gamers, not superheroes like the Indestructibles—sit down to play a game and end up trapped in another world filled with magic and monsters?

For starters, they won't find getting home as easy.

For another: maybe this fantasy game world is where they really belong.

For six lifelong friends, it was supposed to just be a simple game night.

But when they break out a new, classic high-fantasy style game—half tabletop RPG, half dungeon-crawling board game, simultaneously familiar and unexplored—for a test run, they find themselves transported into the game's setting, living the lives of their made-up characters, where the dangers, and the monsters, are deadly serious.

Left with little choice but to jump headlong into their roles, Cordelia, Morgan, Jack, Eriko, Tamsin, and Tobias will have to become the heroes they were just pretending to be to stop a nightmare creature's reign of terror… or find out if life and death in this fictional setting is as real as it seems.

Ranger and cleric, barbarian and thief, bard and magician: they'll have to combine all of their new-found abilities to stop a creeping evil and to survive in this strange new world.

The Dungeon Crawlers novellas, Book 1, *The Players Guide to Dungeon Crawling*, and Book 2, *The Dungeoneer's Bestiary*, are now available in e-book format!

Chapter 1: Game Night

Cordelia sat in her car, watching rain spatter against the glass, shattering the light reflected from Jack's house like bulbs on a Christmas tree. She pulled the hood of her canvas jacket up and took a deep breath, regretting the Chuck Taylors she wore on her feet. I am entirely unprepared for this weather, she thought. Bracing herself, she jumped out of her car, slamming the door behind her, and darted across the street. She ran full speed into Jack's front door, which did not move as she expected it to, hitting it with a heavy thud.

The door opened. Eriko opened it, looking at her sheepishly from beneath her short, black hair, which she'd aggressively parted to one side today in a sort of toppled-over fauxhawk.

"Sorry," she said. "I think I locked it by accident."

Cordelia just sort of groaned an indignant response and stepped inside. She made sure to splash Eriko with the runoff from her coat.

"Thanks, Cordelia," Eriko said.

"I had to repay you for the gift of a concussion you just gave me with the door, pumpkin," Cordelia said. She kicked off her shoes by the front door and stepped inside. She could smell popcorn and what might be one of Tamsin's vegan monstrosities pretending to be cookies. Before she could investigate fully, her vision went completely black.

"What the fuck," she said, reaching up to feel a heavy towel over her head.

"Figured you could use it," Morgan's deep voice said, hinting at laughter. Cordelia pulled the towel off her head and wiped down her face and shoulders.

"Great night for this, huh?" she said, seeing Morgan's shirt and pants were also still showing signs of a wet walk here.

"It'll add to the ambiance," he said.

Together they walked into the dining room, where everyone else had gathered. Jack at the head of the table, looking giddy and anxious—and Cordelia knew exactly why, too, because after years of cajoling, he, Morgan, and Eriko had finally convinced everyone to try out an actual, honest to goodness role playing game, something they'd been doing for years and wanted their whole, tight friendship circle to join in on. Cordelia used to play, before she'd had to take on a second job to make ends meet after the car accident, and if she were being honest with herself, she was excited to get back into it, too. A chance to hang out with her best friends for some cooperative storytelling and forget about the real world for a while? Sounded like a perfect Friday night to her.

The twins were the real newbies, though Eriko was convinced Tamsin and Tobias were going to be instantly addicted. Tamsin never met a story about magic she didn't love, and Tobias, despite talking a big game, was a closet geek of a highly respectable level, though his tastes leaned more toward comics and Star Wars than Dungeons & Dragons or *Lord of the Rings*. True to character, Tobias was absolutely blistering his sister with jokes about bringing vegan cookies to a game night, and she was giving it right back to him.

Morgan handed Cordelia a drink and clinked his own beverage against hers automatically. She shot him a huge smile. I love my friends, she thought. I love these people. And she was so looking forward to this, because she knew they all had worries they needed to escape from. Eriko's mother had passed away recently, though from her playful demeanor, you'd never know it. Morgan was paying off medical bills for his father, and she could always tell when he his mind turned to that when his gaze drifted. Jack, sitting on the back of his chair like a gargoyle, presiding over the table, was on layoff watch at his day job, expecting to be unemployed at any moment. And the twins had some vicious family drama they avoided the details about as much as possible, though whatever was going on there, they'd both been losing weight to an unhealthy degree from worrying, and Tobias always seemed to have something on his mind he couldn't quite put into words.

Money and health; family and jobs. Real world stuff. The real world is cruel and unfair. Give me a fight against a goblin horde and rolling some dice any day instead, Cordelia thought.

"Hey Jack!" Cordelia said. "What game did you decide on? D&D? Pathfinder? Maybe Shadowrun?"

"Oh man, I should've done Shadowrun," Jack said, hoping off his chair. He winked at her. Very few people can wink without looking creepy, and because of this, Jack and Cordelia had spent their entire lives together—classmates since the second grade, friends the entire time—practicing the non-creepy wink. It became a tradition to try to be the first one to wink at the other when they got together, and when possible to make it as creepy as possible. He failed on the creepy part as he tripped over his own feet jumping off his chair and almost face-planted on the table.

"Grace and elegance, as always," Morgan said. "Thank you for not shattering your teeth on the table."

Jack bowed dramatically.

"Thank you, thank you," he said. "That was what we'd call a failed acrobatics check. And to answer your question, Cordie, I've got a new game for us."

"So, what you're saying is we're going to spend the next four hours watching you try to figure out the rules," Eriko said.

"What? No. Well. Maybe?" Jack said. "But there's an upside. No dungeon master. We all get to play."

"Instead of you or Morgan trying to kill us with orcs," Eriko said.

"I have never tried to kill you with orcs," Morgan said.

"No, you prefer things out of forgotten pages of a monster compendium so we don't have any idea what we're fighting," Eriko said.

"True," Morgan said.

"That's why I usually like dragons. You know what you're going to fight, but you know you're going to die anyway," Jack said. "Anyway. This thing's got a sort of... it uses cards and dice roles as an AI."

Jack slid the box onto the table, a big, dense cube of cardboard emblazoned with stereotypical high fantasy art. Morgan pulled it in front of him.

"Where'd you pick this up?" he asked.

"Dragon Forge," Jack said.

"I love how you guys basically speak an entire language of your own," Tobias said, eyeballing the box from opposite Morgan.

"And yet you understand every word we say," Eriko said.

"I am fluent in geek," Tobias said. "I judge not."

"Dragon Forge, huh?" Morgan said.

"Yeah. Lonnie's knocking prices down on everything. Trying to clear out stock so he doesn't have to throw anything out when they close," Jack said.

Cordelia picked up on the wistful tone between Jack and Morgan. The game shop downtown had been there since they were kids, but it had been dying a slow death for years. Lack of interest and online sales were killing the small store.

"Okay, I don't speak geek," Tamsin said. "But I'd like a translation. What's going on with this?"

"Usually one of us directs the game and everyone else plays a character," Cordelia said. "Correction – usually Jack or Morgan directs the game, depending on the campaign. And it's like collaborative storytelling."

"You of all people are going to love this," Tobias said to his sister.

"And you're not?" she said back.

"I am open to the experience," he said. "God knows I've heard you guys talking about it for enough years. Might as well actually participate. I feel like this is some part of your life I've never met before. It's like meeting your Mr. Snuffleupagus."

"So, in this case, everyone picks a type of character," Jack said. "The game sort of tells us how the villains react, so we can all be on the same side. Which is a nice change of pace for us."

"And probably a little better for you since we know how much you love confrontation," Eriko said. The doorbell rang, and she darted off. "Pizza's here."

"I really don't like competitive games," Tamsin said.

"Well, I mean, RPGs really aren't intended to be competitive. We're all on the same side to tell the story. But…" Jack said.

"It'll be nice for everyone to play a character for once," Morgan said.

"You're not going to miss playing the all-powerful game master?" Cordelia said.

"You know how much extra work that is!" Morgan said. "No. I'm not going to miss it."

Eriko re-entered and slid three boxes of pizza onto the table.

"Who ordered?" Eriko said.

"Me," Jack said.

"You hungry when you ordered?" Eriko said.

"Maybe," Jack said.

"Because this is overkill," Eriko said.

"First rule of ordering pizza. Don't order when you're already hungry," he replied, sliding the box open, revealing map pieces, dice, and little plastic miniatures in the shape of monsters and heroes.

"Dibs on the rogue," Eriko said.

"Always," Cordelia said. "Have you ever played anything else?"

"I was that multiclass rogue-sorcerer that one time," Eriko said.

"I sometimes wonder how you didn't end up in a life of crime," Cordelia said.

"Who… do I pick who I play?" Tamsin said, gingerly poking through a pile of gray heroic figurines. "Oh, this one's got a book. This one's mine."

"Least surprising moment of the night, ladies and gentlemen," Eriko said. "Tamsin wants to play the wizard."

"Ravenclaw for life, babe," Tamsin said. "You going to try to convince me I shouldn't play a magician?"

"I was going to suggest it if you didn't figure it out for yourself," Eriko said.

"I am so being the dude with the guitar," Tobias said, holding up a figure, vaguely elven in look, with a sword in one hand and a lute in the other.

"Why are you pretending you don't know that's a bard?" Morgan said.

"Because I keep forgetting I'm in friendly company, among my fellow geeks," Tobias said. "Bard it is. Tell me this means I've got magic songs."

"I think you have magic songs," Jack said, lifting a hand up in the air to catch something Morgan threw at him. His face lit up. "You know me so well, Morgan."

"We have had approximately seven hundred conversations about how you miss playing a ranger in the past year," Morgan said. He picked up another piece and slide it across the table. "Yours even comes with a wolf pet."

"Oh, this is so amazingly stereotypical and I love it," Jack said. "I love playing the stereotypical ranger! It's my favorite overused archetype!"

Tobias took his miniature and put it down next to his sister's.

"Look, Tam. We're even twins in the game. Team pointy ears!"

He held a hand up for a high five. His sister left him hanging there for a full fifteen seconds before begrudgingly slapping his palm with her own.

"Of course you guys are elves," Eriko said.

"What? Why do you say that?" Tamsin said.

"Because elves are pretty, and the two of you are fucking gorgeous in real life," Eriko said. "You're just staying true to form."

"I am choosing to take that as a compliment," Tobias said. "And I will not be persuaded otherwise."

Eriko turned her figurine over in her hand, scoping out the design.

"These are bizarrely nice for a game I've never heard of," she said. "I'm calling my character Rouge, by the way."

"Rouge the Rogue," Morgan deadpanned.

"Come on, you know that's funny," she said. "The internet spells it that way all the time. I'll be the most famous rogue on the interwebs!"

"Basically your life's goal, in real life or otherwise," Jack said. "Who you got, Cordie?"

Cordelia rummaged through the remaining heroes. There were plenty of options—a heavily armored knight, a druidic priestess, some sort of alchemist, someone who looked like a combination of warrior and magician. Then she found the one she knew she had to play. She set it down on the table proudly.

"That is boss," Eriko said.

"That's terrifying," Tamsin said.

"What is that?" Morgan said, picking the piece up. "Oh dude, you're a barbarian!"

"An orc barbarian, if I'm looking at that correctly," Cordelia said.

"Might be a half-orc," Jack said, sliding a card across the table with her character's stats. The card also had a portrait of the character in full color—green-skinned, with a reddish Mohawk, slightly pointed hears, and fierce fangs visible where her lower canine teeth would be. She carried a battle axe almost as tall as she was.

"I think I love this character already," Cordelia said.

"You're playing a monster then," Tamsin said.

"A good monster," Tobias said. "This is why we love you, Cordelia."

"A badass monster woman with an axe and a Mohawk who is going to slay all the critters that try to get you guys," Cordelia said. "I'm basically *Lord of the Rings* She-Hulk."

"Feeling the need to smash some stuff to blow off some steam?" Tobias said.

"You got it," Cordelia sad.

"What about you, big guy?" Eriko said, punching Morgan in the arm. "Paladin? Deathknight? Necromancer?"

Morgan poked around the pile of figures until he found a solidly built character in heavy armor with a two-handed hammer in his hands.

"Group needs a cleric," he said. "I'll volunteer to be den mother."

"Not every group needs a healer," Jack said. "We've played without one before."

Morgan laughed his infectious laugh.

"This motley group needs a healer," he said. "Trust me, I bet we'll all be glad I'm playing this guy before the first session is over."

"Rogue, cleric, barbarian, wizard, with a ranger and a freakazoid bard thrown in for good measure," Eriko said. "Good group. I like it."

"Do we name them?" Tamsin said.

"Oh, please tell me we get to name them," Tobias said.

Jack was thumbing through the instructions, nodding to himself.

"It's a campaign," he said. "We'll play the same characters through a whole bunch of sessions. Absolutely you should name them. It's part of the story. We already have Rouge already."

"Please tell me that's not canon," Morgan said.

"I picked the game. I say it's canon," Jack said.

Eriko stuck her tongue out at Morgan. Morgan pretended to try to grab it.

"I'm going to name my guy…" Tobias started.

"Please don't be super snarky about it," Cordelia pleaded.

"Oberon the Blue," Tobias said.

"That is… not super snarky," Cordelia said.

"It almost sounds like a bard name," Morgan said.

"Then I'll be Nimue the Silver," Tamsin said.

"Oh, it's like you guys have been doing this your whole lives," Jack said, clutching his hands to his chest. "I am so proud of you."

"Are you serious about Rouge?" Morgan asked Eriko, sounding resigned.

"Can it be my nickname, at least?" Eriko said.

"Fine, I guess," Morgan said.

"Okay, Rouge the Rogue. My given name is Scarlet."

"Oh, come on!" Morgan said, sending Eriko into a belly laugh. "What about you, chief?"

"I'm going all in on the ridiculous stereotypes," Jack said. "I'll just introduce my character as Raven."

Now it was Morgan's turn to roar laughing.

"Man, you are just diving right into the fantasy ranger trope machine, huh?"

"We never do tropes! We try so hard not to do tropes," Jack said. "I say for Tam and Tobias' first game, we just own it."

"Fine," Morgan said. "I'll call my cleric Bastion."

"So melodramatic!" Jack said.

"Hey, you said we're gonna own it," Morgan said. "If you're all in, I'm all in."

"You guys were going to give me a hard time about not coming up with a good name, and you're Raven and Bastion?" Tobias said. "You're like, walking terrible fan fic right now."

"And proud of it," Morgan said. "What about you, Cordelia? Are you the Widowmaker? The Deathdealer?"

"Orchid," Cordelia said.

Everyone went silent for a moment.

"Orchid... the orc," Eriko said. "I just want to go on record that nobody gets to make fun of me for this entire campaign when she's playing Orchid the orc."

Cordelia let a vast smile creep across her face.

"Orchids are ridiculously delicate. They're hard to keep alive. And I'm playing a battle-scarred barbarian warrior. I think it's pretty damned clever, what I just did right there."

"It really is," Tamsin said. She raised her glass in the air. "To Orchid the orc!"

"I love you guys," Cordelia said. "So, we have characters, we have names, we have pizza... how do we start?"

Jack picked up the oddly shaped dice from the box and hefted them in the palm of his hand.

"These look weird to you? They're... They look like they're six sided, but there's something not right about them. Like they're not balanced correctly."

Eriko took one from him and held it up to her eye.

"Are they melted? You're right, this doesn't look balanced."

Morgan took one as well.

"They aren't plastic," he said. "They don't feel like something that would melt. Like stone?"

"Whatever," Eriko said. She juggled her lone die in her hand. "Let's see how they roll, anyway."

She tossed the die onto the table.

And then everyone disappeared.

Other books by Matthew Phillion

the Indestructibles series
the Indestructibles
Breakout (Book 2)
the Entropy of Everything (Book 3)
Like a Comet (Book 4)

Also set in the Indestructibles Universe
Echo and the Sea

One-Shots (shorts and novellas)
Gifted
The Soloist
The Monsters We Make
Blood & Bone
Krampus in the City

The Dungeon Crawlers series of novellas
The Players Guide to Dungeon Crawling
The Dungeoneer's Bestiary

ABOUT THE AUTHOR

Matthew Phillion is a writer, actor, and film director based in Salem, Massachusetts and the author of the Indestructibles Young Adult superhero adventure series, its spinoff, Echo and the Sea, and the newly launched Dungeon Crawlers series.

An active freelance writer, Phillion writes about healthcare, pop culture, and more. He enjoys adventuring with his sidekick, Watson the terrier mutt, and is also the official manservant to his very demanding cat Harley.

Made in the USA
Middletown, DE
26 August 2018